Persuaded

A Great Lakes Story

by Inez Ross

Ashley House

Published by Ashley House
614 47th Street
Los Alamos, New Mexico 87544

ISBN:978-9664337-4-2-4

Library of Congress Control Number:
2001 129090

Second edition 2010

Printed in Canada

All characters in this work are fictitious, but resemblance to characters in other works of fiction may be intentional.

Names of some locations are actual; some are fictional; some have been moved for purposes of the story.

Maps are not to scale.

Some legends in this story have been adapted from the versions in *Were-Wolves* and *Will-O-The-Wisps: French Tales of Mackinac Retold* by Dirk Gringhuis Published by the Mackinac Island State Park Commission

Thanks to Secundino Sandoval for cover art, John Cole for graphic design, and James Hemsing for technical assistance.

The author wishes to thank these editor friends for their suggestions and encouragement:
Lynette, Lois, Lucille, Dexter, and Phyllis

And thanks to Jane for plot ideas and the reminder to keep laughing at ourselves as well as at our neighbors

Chapter I

In the eighteenth century the ancient family of Eliot migrated to the New World.

In the nineteenth century they found that their investments in land and minerals gave them more power and prestige in America than their noble titles had afforded them in England.

But in the twentieth century the dynasty had dwindled, and the loss of fortune and status corresponded with the shrinking size of the family in which fewer male heirs remained to continue the family name.

In a recent year on one cold March afternoon in Michigan's Upper Peninsula, Ann Eliot, one of the three remaining daughters who still bore the Eliot name, stood inside the door of Woodleigh Hall, preparing to go for a run before dinner.

She opened the big door and gasped as the cold air hit her face. Her breath was visible and a chill ran down her arms. She had doubts about attempting her usual five-mile loop. It had been many months since she had run that far, and with the cloudy sky it was impossible to tell how soon the lowering twilight would end in complete darkness.

It felt right to be at home again in the Upper Peninsula, but the unpacking and the family conversations had taken the better part of the day and deferred until almost dark her opportunity to be in the forest.

As she started out, she recalled how much she loved the huge white pines which soared above her like pillars in a cathedral. In the summer the maple understory would filter the sunlight and the air would be all green and golden. But now the atmosphere was a soft gray, lightened only by the fine snow which filtered slowly down. Spring arrives late in northern Michigan.

Her next concern was Trapper, the huge dog she would have to encounter on the road near Uppercross Cottage. Her brother-in-law was proud of the big brown animal which so ably guarded the gatehouse, but she dreaded meeting the rambunctious animal whose barking would call attention to her and whose playful leaps could almost knock her down. Ann's running suit bore tiny holes as evidence of the dog's playful nips.

A long stick was usually the best deterrent against the dog's advances, but looking for one would mean stopping to search in the snow. The road bore no marks of traffic, the gateway yard looked empty, and the fading afternoon was wrapped in deep snow-flannel quiet. She hoped that Trapper would remain asleep in the doghouse, allowing her to run by undetected. Only the soft crunch of the snow under her shoes would indicate her presence. Taking the far side of the road and increasing her pace, she passed the doghouse successfully and reached the boundary of the gatehouse property.

Just as she was slowing to a more comfortable pace, a sight in the distance caused her heart to beat more rapidly again. The figure of another runner could barely be discerned on the road ahead. It was impossible in the snow and gathering twilight to identify him unquestionably, but the height, the stride, the way he moved his arms, all said Frederick Wentworth.

She could not catch up to him at her present pace, but in order to identify him positively, she could take the cutoff path through the forest, and if he continued north on the St Ambrose Road, she would meet him near Simon Slough.

The challenge of having a goal was enjoyable and her speed increased, but she began to laugh at herself. She must be hallucinating. She hadn't seen Frederick Wentworth in five years.

She remembered that summer, which seemed so long ago, when she had lived in the Eliot Bluff Cottage on Big Turtle Island with her Aunt Nettie and had taken a job as waitress at the Grand Hotel there. During the Lilac Festival the kitchen crew had challenged the wait crew to enter the footrace. At the top of the hill, jumping aside to let a horse-drawn carriage go by, she had stepped off the road and sprained her ankle. Frederick, returning along the course in a cooldown run, was her hero rescuer, helping her down the hill and carrying her into the first-aid tent.

There was never a more classic example of love at first sight. The appearance, interests, and situation of each so suited the other that a period of exquisite happiness followed. He was four years older than she was. That summer he was carriage driver and stable hand. Ann enjoyed riding along next to him on the high front seat as they took tourists from the ferry landing up the hill to the Grand Hotel.

As she ran through the pine forest on this wintry spring day, she recalled the smell of lilacs, the sunshine, and the blue water of the Straits of Mackinac where he had taken her sailing.

Romantic fluff! That's what her Aunt Jewell and Aunt Nettie had called their friendship. And even though the couple had committed themselves to a permanent attachment, her aunt had reminded her that July romances are as ephemeral as summer fog. Aunt Jewell especially had deprecated the connection in every way. Ann Eliot, at seventeen, to commit herself to a man with no fortune or career? It must not be! Ann was persuaded to see the imprudence of an early engagement by the person whom she had loved and relied on since her mother's death. Aunt Jewell had a horror of anything approaching imprudence, and Ann consented to changing the relationship to one of friendly correspondence.

Frederick did not agree. He had been so warmly attached that her decision disappointed him deeply, and he charged her with yielding too easily to persuasion. He accused her of a weakness in character and lack of independent spirit, as if she were giving him up only to oblige others. Deeply angered, he at first wanted a complete break, but Ann prevailed in obtaining at least his promise to write to her at college.

Aunt Jewell was as clever as she was firm. She suggested that if they were to write to each other that Frederick should be the one to begin the correspondence. Having heard that Frederick associated with a frivolous set of comrades, she was convinced that any promise of his would be only a capricious commitment, taken lightly and easily broken. Aunt Jewell believed that he would forget Ann by the end of summer.

Ann agreed to that challenge and convinced Frederick to write first. But, though she had his promise, no communication followed. The summer ended, and Ann returned to college. She eventually broke her resolve and wrote to him. She sent a postcard reminding him of her address and phone number at the university. But no answer ever came. Her attachment and regrets were eventually repressed by her immersion in academic studies. She formed other friendships, but no one had ever come within her social circle who could bear a comparison with Frederck Wentworth as he stood in her memory.

Darkness was approaching as Ann emerged from the forest on the St. Ambrose Road. She stopped to catch her breath, and removed her hat and gloves to cool off. She loved the touch of the snow on her face and stuck out her tongue to taste some flakes. But she saw no other person, runner or otherwise. Perhaps she had been too slow, even with the shortcut, and he had already gone by. She examined the road carefully, looking for footprints. But unless she had been immediately behind him, the falling snow would have obliterated any tracks. Perhaps he had taken another route or turned back. She decided that the increasing darkness and the falling snow was making senseless any further waiting, and she turned away from the road to take the lane and complete the loop home.

Darkness was now complete, and only the ambient whiteness of the snow indicated the lane through the trees toward the Hall. A dark shape moved across her path and slunk into the woods. Too small for a deer and too sinuous for a coyote, it had to be a giant cat. Her fatigue and the increasing chill reminded her of the danger of her position and made the thought of home seem extra inviting.

The experience of the ghostly sighting of Frederick and her pursuit of him must be a reaction inspired by the relief of having finished her studies, and of completing her thesis. She was regressing into romance! The coming spring and summer would bring her down to earth with the reality of job searching and new pursuits, but meanwhile the magic of the forest and the comfort of home were delights that would soothe.

The last mile of the approach to home was easier. She soon saw the lighted windows of Woodleigh Hall. Her elder sister Elizabeth met her at the door.

"What took you so long? Aunt Jewell was ready to send out a search party for you."

"I was chasing a phantom, but couldn't catch him."

"I'll bet it was the Red Dwarf," Elizabeth replied. "Remember Aunt Nettie said he's the phantom that always brings bad news, and you're about to hear some from Aunt Jewell."

Chapter II

Mrs. Henry Von Russett, nee Jewell Eliot, of Forest County, Michigan, was a woman who, for her own amusement, seldom took up any book but her great Bible. That choice was not due to zealous piety, but to the comfort she received in perusing the extensive genealogical chart of her own family contained in the pages between the Old and New Testaments of that heavy tome.

When distressed by the world situation, she pored over the lists showing the original Colonial land grants. When unsettled by domestic affairs, she scanned the remnants of her ancestry in England, and when seeking occupation for an idle hour, she took great pleasure in the page which reaffirmed her position as one of the elite of her society, one of the few persons who could trace her roots to ancient nobility and who maintained the dignity of her position as a proud American matriarch.

Status and propriety were the beginning and end of Jewell Von Russett's character, status based on old family and old money. The Eliots of England were obliged to leave their titles of nobility behind when they became a part of the New World, but they continued to live as landed gentry and invested wisely in property, timber, and minerals. Her great grandfather had been a lumber baron in Michigan's Upper Peninsula but had wisely reserved a large tract of land for his family estate, and now Jewell found herself as owner and mistress of the large manor house on an enclave within the Ojibwa National Forest, an estate which contained one of the few remaining stands of virgin white pine trees in the state. And because of the wisely invested fortune of her forebears, she and her husband were able to live, until only recently, quite comfortably on the interest of her holdings and maintain a lifestyle befitting her dignity.

Sitting in the library of Woodleigh Hall on this March afternoon, she ran her fingers lovingly down the last page of the big book, touching her own name and that of the man she had married twenty-five years before. When they first met, she had seen Henry Von

Russett as quite impecunious and displaying an overabundance of freckles, but he had a fine head of red hair, a merry laugh, and a pedigree nearly as good as her own. He was descended from the Von Russetts who were among the earliest Dutch settlers of old New Amsterdam and was connected on the maternal side with Diedrich Knickerbocker himself.

Their marriage was a comfortable one. He had grown portly and arthritic, but still enjoyed playing cards and going shooting with the hunters of the nearby villages, while she followed her genealogical and charitable pursuits. They stayed out of each other's way for the most part, having the space available to those of large income and commodious living quarters, but they presented a united facade to the public with their common interest of entertaining the important families of the county. They enjoyed seeing each other from opposite ends of the long table in the great hall when it was loaded with venison pies and surrounded by a laughing group of deer hunters or the studious members of the Yoopers Family Tree Society.

The final lines of the family chart listed the names of her most recent concern, the death, ten years before, of her brother Walter and the subsequent adoption of his three daughters, Mary, Elizabeth, and Ann. Already a widower, Walter Eliot had prided himself on his youthful appearance and was even more intensely proud of his heritage than his sister was. His only regret was that, lacking any male issue, the name of Eliot could not continue. He would see his daughters well situated, of course, but he had been thinking of remarriage for himself in order to continue the family name.

Now this responsibility of seeing the daughters well married had descended to Jewell. She took on the task with a decided fervor. Her commitment was made more serious with the realization that the family coffers, although adequate for herself and her husband could not extend much longer into the future for the education and support of impoverished nieces.

Mary, the eldest at twenty seven, had acquired a little importance by becoming Mrs. Charles Musgrove, the eldest son of a man whose landed property and general consequence made him second only to the Von Russetts in the county. Mary and Charles with their two children lived in the Gatehouse Cottage, actually a smaller version of the huge Huntingdon Lodge occupied by his parents and sisters.

Elizabeth, twenty-five, the middle daughter, was still unmarried, attractive, proud, sociable, but with no serious prospects for a husband or career. She had spent a year at a fashionable finishing school in New York and had learned how to carry on a conversation, to coordinate her makeup and costume colors, and to enter a room gracefully, but she had no inclination for mathematics, business, or serious reading. She was content to live in the west wing of Woodleigh Hall, drive her convertible to shopping centers, dance with friends at local roadhouses, and read magazines that featured movie stars and British royalty. She presently was hostess to a friend, Penny Clay, who had been staying at Woodleigh Hall for several weeks. Jewell approved accepting long-term guests such as Penny, in the tradition of the great houses of old-country gentry, but she thought Penny a dangerous influence and disproved of the frivolous life the young women led. Their most serious pursuits seemed to consist of polishing their nails and drying their hair.

But Jewell maintained one hope that could still offer a solution. When Elizabeth had been in grammar school, her father had obtained the address of a distant cousin, William Eliot, with whom Elizabeth had established correspondence as a penpal. The families had never met, but Jewell was given to understand that the Eliots of Virginia were well-favored, wealthy, and powerful. The correspondence, in the manner of most rapidly shifting interests of youth, had soon died out and contact had been lost many years ago. But a recent exchange of letters with a genealogical acquaintance in New Jersey had brought the young man to light again. He was rumored to be an Oxford graduate, personable, wealthy, and as yet unmarried. Jewell was waiting for the answer to her letter inviting him to visit at Woodleigh Hall.

And Ann, twenty-two, the youngest daughter, who had just completed her studies in art history at university, needed an introduction into a wider society if she were ever going to make any marriage at all. She had grown thin and serious with her academic life, and Jewell felt that a change would improve Ann's spirits and appearance. She had spent one summer living on Big Turtle Island with Jewell's sister Nettie in the great bluff cottage Nettie owned there, but she had insisted on working at the

Grand Hotel with common young people whom Jewell and Nettie considered to be beneath Ann's social class.

And the newly arisen problem of financial difficulty must first be addressed. Jewell suspected that the recent decline in the family bank account was somehow connected with Henry's increasing attraction to the Native American casinos with his group of men friends who made weekly visits there, but two considerations had prevented her from raising any outward objection.

First, in maintaining the appearance of comfortably situated gentry, she thought it natural that her lord of the manor not be associated with employment or business matters other than those of the estate. It was to be expected that such a man should occupy his time with hunting and be able to cover a few losses at cards.

And then, even though she was actually in charge of the family, her traditions told her that Henry should appear to be the one in control. She abhorred the possibility of Henry's being like a consort, trailing behind the queen with his hands behind him. And so clever had she been in presenting the proper picture to family and friends, so tactful in only suggesting and recommending policies to her husband, that even he believed that he was the ruling head of the household, attended by a dutiful wife.

But although her fears due to the decreasing available cash had prompted her hints and questions to become less subtle, Henry had not shared her concern and summarily dismissed the review of the accounts with a wave of the hand. The summer loomed ahead involving the entertainment of the two unmarried nieces and a guest, plus the increased social obligations of the season. What to do? Somehow, they must retrench. Her head ached at the thought of choosing any one area where expenses could be cut back.

But, the matter must come out, and in an unprecdented move, she decided to put the question openly to the family this very evening at dinner.

The bell rang, summoning the family to the evening meal and rousing Jewell from her reverie. She closed the book, and looking into the gilt-framed mirror, she patted the waves of her iron gray hair, gathered the aplomb and dignity which her handsome appearance always reinforced, then made her way to the great hall for dinner.

Chapter III

Woodleigh Hall, even though situated in a clearing on a pleasant rise of ground, concealed its grandeur from travelers on the main road by its situation a half mile into the extensive pine forest at the end of a winding drive. The huge timber and stone mansion resembled the massive lodges built early in the last century in some of the western national parks, and the dark logs and stone chimneys along with the low outbuildings of the same design gave a rustic and picturesque air to the forest clearing.

In the commodious room which served as both dining hall and ballroom several trophy heads of animals looked down from a balcony extending three quarters of the way around the room, evidence of Henry's success on various safaris. The staring heads and the huge stone fireplace gave the room the character of a medieval banqueting hall, an impression at odds with the Regency table setting with its delicate china and silver candle holders.

Jewell Von Russett sat at the foot and her husband at the head of the long table. The choice of this secondary position for Jewell was not only due to the deference for her husband's rank, but also to her own preference that the ugly boar's head with its giant tusks which hung over the entrance door remain out of sight at her back. She preferred to face instead the gigantic moose head which graced the head of the hall over the fireplace. Henry enjoyed sitting beneath it, his back to the fire, looking down the long narrow table as a lord of the manor should. And he enjoyed operating the mechanical contrivances he had installed throughout the house. From his chair he now handled a remote control which raised and lowered the chandelier, seeking the right amount of light for the table, until Jewell told him to stop.

Ann entered the great hall with trepidation at Elizabeth's warning of bad news and politely begged forgiveness for appearing in exercise clothing instead of changing for dinner as was the rule. But as she seated herself opposite Penny and Elizabeth, she noted that the chill in the room was repeated in the silence and in the air of strained stiffness evident with the diners.

Noting the length of the table and the extra space between the family members, Ann asked, "Are we all angry at each other that we have to sit so far apart? "

"Serle forgot to take the extra leaves out of the table after last night's supper meeting," explained Jewell. "I've spoken to him about it."

The silence descended again and Ann noted that something must have occurred to create the atmosphere of negative tension that seemed to prevail. Henry appeared red-faced and embarrassed, Jewell was glaring at him with compressed lips and lowered brows. Elizabeth, with her accustomed cool composure, picked up her dessert spoon and focused on the pudding before her, but Penny sat quietly with her hands in her lap, her dark lashes sparkling with a few tears which fell onto her plump cheeks.

Penny, though quite shy, was as a rule very cheerful, and her effervescent spirits, combined with Henry's risible comments, usually made the dining hour a merry interlude.

Penny Clay, nee Penelope Shepherd, had returned to the Upper Peninsula after an unprosperous marriage and had found consolation in her friendship with Elizabeth. It was hinted that she may have had a child of whom she had lost custody but for whose sake she retained her married name, even though she still cringed at being referred to as Mrs. Clay.

"I think it is time I went home," she said softly. "Now that Ann is here she will want the west bedroom."

Her statement received immediate negation from all four of the others. "Oh, not yet, Penny!" remarked Elizabeth. "Spring is coming and we have so many pleasant outings planned."

"No," Ann chimed in. "My room has always been the dormer on the east side. Besides, we have so many bedrooms here we could accommodate an army."

Henry's response was the most vociferous. "Absolutely not. We would be considered paupers for sure if we had to turn away our most privileged visitor. We would give up any number of pleasures before cutting back on hospitality. We enjoy Penny's company too much to let her go."

Jewell agreed. "My Dear, you must pardon me for bringing up a delicate family matter in your presence. Our little difficulties are only temporary and in no way connected to your visit. You must not leave us before the end of the summer."

So it was a question of finances that had produced the gloom, deduced Ann. The stipend furnished for her university education had been more than adequate, and by the end of summer she would have employment that would enable her to be self supporting, but she knew she must avoid proposing summer employment to bridge the gap. Her experience of working on the Island five years ago had caused such objections from Jewell and from Jewell's sister Nettie that she had not dared to suggest another summer like it. Jewell and Nettie lived in the past, Ann thought, and truly in a different world. They would have her preserved like a doll on a shelf until presented as a debutante in their society world, a world which now consisted only of a few ageing chatelaines and spinster aunts.

Why couldn't Elizabeth find a career that would offer gainful employment? Ann felt that Elizabeth could be a successful fashion model or even a television actress, but Aunt Jewell must be saving her for some wealthy doctor or software mogul who would sweep her away to a private life of privilege and ease.

The coffee was brought in to end the meal, and only the soft clink of delicate cups on saucers punctuated the silence until a sound from outside indicated entering visitors.

Charles Musgrove, Mary's husband, fairly barged into the room in consequence of being almost dragged by the big brown Trapper, who was straining at the leash and bounding in happy anticipation of investigating the humans and the dinner smells of the great hall. Hearing the welcome of the host, the dog headed for Henry's chair, and as Henry rose, proceeded to jump up and put huge paws on Henry's shoulders.

"Well, hello there, Trapper," laughed Henry. "Welcome to Woodleigh Hall. This is a rare and happy visit for sure." And unsnapping the leash, he stood up and grabbed the huge paws as if shaking hands or preparing to dance with the lumbering creature. Trapper responded by licking Henry's face and then bounding around the room in great leaps, encouraged by the laughter and genial greetings from the diners. The atmosphere expanded to merriment until a crystal bon-bon dish went tumbling from the sideboard and shattered on the stone floor. At the same time everyone saw that Charles' discomfiture was due to something other than the dog's rambunctious behavior. He managed to restrain the animal, attach the leash, and secure the dog in the anteroom before returning with apologies and news of a most somber nature.

"We have just received word that Aunt Nettie has passed away."

Chapter IV

Henry Von Russett was caught in an unhappy dilemma. Sitting in his timbered den in Woodleigh Hall amidst the unopened packages of his latest purchase, he smoothed back his thinning red hair and pondered his problem.

Perhaps the present difficulty was due to his penchant for purchasing gadgetry. He had always been fascinated by gimmickry and mechanical toys, and up to now, he never had need to consider budget limitations. He had acquired an immense variety of historical and modern mechanisms. The study was crammed with everything from chronometers, high-power spotting scopes, anti-gravity magnets, and remote controlled robots, to ancient astrolabes, old cameras, and antique brass telescopes. Because it was easier to acquire the newer items than to search catalogs and shops for the older items, his collection was weighted increasingly toward the more recent technology. And computing machines, especially, seemed to grow obsolete in such a short period of time, that it became necessary to replace them continually with the newer and more expensive models. An example was the array of boxes he now stared at containing a new machine of higher power than his outdated one, accompanied by a printer, a scanner, and several other accessories he believed were necessary to complete the set.

His real problem, only dimly perceived perhaps, was his early life as an over-indulged and over-directed only child with a smothering and autocratic mother. His pliable and amenable nature had been trained to yield to edicts by his superiors, so that after the death of his mother, it seemed quite comfortable for him to marry a woman of means who could continue to furnish all the material comforts as well as make all the major decisions. Jewell Von Russett was the power behind his throne.

He realized that Jewell knew how to run the business of the family from behind the scenes. Indeed, so tactful was she that her consultations with him left him feeling he had made wise and astute decisions. Until today.

She had this morning displayed the ledgers and documents that Mr. Shepherd, her agent and attorney, had drawn out, showing the necessity for retrenchment in their expenditures. She had never breathed a hint of an objection to his considerable gaming losses at the casinos, to his purchase of the new high-powered hunting rifle that graced his gun cabinet or to the extra saddle horse that had raised the feed and veterinary bills.

The memory of that embarrassing evening when she had asked at dinner for the family to suggest ways to retrench had finally pierced his indifference, and the recollection had stayed with him like a morsel of undigested food. He belched briefly at the thought.

Nettie's death he had at first thought would be the solution to the problem. Eliot Bluff Cottage on Big Turtle Island was a three-story Victorian mansion, and Jewell was the sole inheritor. But instead of putting it up for sale or planning to rent it to wealthy vacationers from Detroit or Chicago who were always looking for an elegant retreat, she had happily announced that after disposing of or re-arranging Nettie's possessions, which she was at this time doing, she would be moving there herself for the summer.

Elizabeth and Ann had expressed a desire to accompany her, but Henry declared that he preferred to remain in the forest at Woodleigh Hall.

The sound of horse's feet on the drive wakened him from his reverie, and opening the window, he espied Charles Musgrove and an unknown passenger riding in Charles' little two-wheeled red cart behind the bay mare. Henry knew that Charles' parents must have a new guest at Huntingdon Lodge because the new visitors usually preferred the novelty of sightseeing by horse carriage rather than touring by car.

"Come on up, Charles, but don't bring the dog," he called down to them, then laughed as they remembered the dining hall scene.

"Trapper stayed home this time," Charles replied. "But I have a friend who is taking a neighborhood tour and would like to meet you."

Henry cordially invited them up and Charles presented his guest, an Admiral

Croft from Duluth, Minnesota.

Admiral Croft was a short swarthy man with black curly hair, smiling and affable, wearing a Navy pea-coat and captain's kepi. Newly retired, he was staying with his wife at Huntingdon Lodge, where Charles helped his parents by being a hunting guide and a general tour escort.

Admiral Croft looked around with curiosity at the collection of clocks and mechanical contrivances that crowded the study, and just as Henry offered him a chair, the room came alive with ringing, banging, twittering, and gonging sounds. All the clocks, from the tall grandfather clock to the cuckoo and talking clocks, announced the hour of two p.m. The Admiral jumped up from the chair, startled, not merely because of the sudden cacophony, but also because his chair had begun to shake.

Charles laughed and said, "I warned you, didn't I Admiral, about what you might find here!"

And Henry, with an apology mixed with a modicum of pride switched off the electric massage mechanism of the chair and explained his hobby. As he did so, a little robot with spherical head and flashing green eyes tottered across the room extending a wire arm which ended in a white-gloved hand holding a cigar. The Admiral laughed and said, "No, thank you. I don't smoke."

Henry had found a delighted listener. The next hour was an exploration of the intricate contrivances lining the room and demonstrations of their various operations, ending with the unpacking of the new computer boxes and an excited discussion of the machine and all its accessories.

Henry grew more expansive regarding the automatic devices he had installed throughout the house and offered to show their guest through the entire Hall to see, among other things, the mechanism which lowered and raised the great hall chandelier, the spring-operated secret panel in the library, and the remote controlled talking front door device.

The Admiral was enchanted. "This would be an ideal place for my council to meet on their study weekend," he said. "Is there any possibility of your renting out part of your home for the month of August?"

A light went on in Henry's mind, and as they continued to discuss the possibilites, the munificent leasing-fee offer expanded to become a lucrative amount, the time in question expanded to become the entire summer, and the space available for rental expanded to encompass the entire estate of Woodleigh. Henry explained that, of course, he had been planning to join his wife and nieces at Big Turtle Island for the summer and the Admiral would be welcome to take possession on Memorial Day weekend. Henry Von Russett and the Admiral closed the discussion with a hearty handshake, promising to meet with Mr. Shepherd at the earliest opportunity to discuss the terms of the lease and draw up the final details of the agreement.

As the little red cart rolled away down the road, Henry sank back in the de-activated massage chair in stupefied self-amazement. He had arranged a major business deal without consulting Jewell, and the transaction left him exhausted.

Chapter V

The shock to Jewell on learning of her sister Nettie's death was no greater than that of learning that Henry had contracted to rent Woodleigh Hall without first consulting her in the matter.

Although Nettie's death was completely unexpected, her health having been assured as sound only a fortnight ago by her doctor, the acquisition of Eliot Bluff Cottage went a long way toward assuaging Jewell's grief. The two sisters had been in close communication, but their sibling rivalry had continued more than three score years, and their phone calls to each other, while replete with an exchange of news and gossip, sometimes ended with snide questions or comments that were quite disparaging.

Nettie had envied the larger estate that Jewell possessed, but Jewell felt the stricture of Nettie's rank as the uncrowned queen of

Turtle Island society. Nettie Eliot had been a pillar of the little Trinity Church there, respected as a benefactor of the poor, and admired as the chairperson of all the major committees of the village. Jewell, in taking possession of Bluff Cottage, hoped to inherit also the privileges of her sister's social status on the Island.

Elizabeth and Ann were helping to sort and catalog their Aunt Nettie's smaller possessions and divide them for charity or possible sale, when the word came regarding Henry's agreeement with Admiral Croft. Jewell and Ann caught the early ferry boat back to the peninsula, leaving Elizabeth and Penny at the Island mansion.

Jewell's stunned reaction to the proposed rental of Woodleigh was at first quite negative. Release her home with its precious paintings, first-edition book collection, and Sevres china to a stranger? It was a horrible thought. Even though the disclosure of the large sum to accrue from the transaction and the knowledge of the Admiral's high rank tended to mollify her fears, she decided to ask Mr. Shepherd for a background check of the lessee's character and assets.

Henry deemed such a drastic move completely unnecessary and answered all her doubts with sweeping reassurances as she listed each objection. What references did he furnish? He was a retired Admiral; there was no questioning his integrity. What about children? The Crofts had none; Jewell's precious objects d'art would be safe. What about hunting privileges? Henry had heard that he sometimes took out a gun, but never killed; quite the gentleman. A more unobjectionable tenant in all essentials could hardly be found.

It was at tea in the library the following week that Jewell confronted Henry with Mr. Shepherd's findings. Admiral Croft was not an admiral at all, but a retired captain of a Great Lakes freighter. And the "council" he wanted to bring to Woodleigh was an assembly of deacons from a Detroit church promoting vacations for inner city children. Jewell blanched in horror at the thought of Woodleigh Hall being overrun by a mob of uncivilized urchins from a ghetto, and she shuddered at the possibility of the clapping and stomping as the council led raucous gospel songs in the sedate environs of Woodleigh Hall. It must not be.

"But, my Dear," remonstrated Henry, "the

good china will be kept locked away, my hunting trophies are high out of reach, and all your little crystal figurines can be removed to the north nook room before we leave."

"The books here are on open shelves," responded Jewell. "I do not want to strip the library and pack hundreds of volumes in boxes. We shall have to lock the library, and certain other parts of the house must remain inaccessible also."

The large library with its leather-covered volumes and graceful decor was a contrast to the rustic medieval great hall. Here amid the rare books and the dignified richness of Regency furniture Jewell was accustomed to serving afternoon tea and receiving important guests. With its gilt-framed ancestral portraits and Persian rugs, the library was the pride and focus of her elegant household.

Ann was present the following afternoon when the Crofts were announced and ushered into the library along with the portly Mr. Shepherd and his battered brown briefcase which he placed on the oak table. Mrs. Croft, a square-built, healthy looking lady with straight short hair and bangs, proved to be as cordial and well spoken as her husband, and her charming manner and obvious delight with the surroundings of the house soon melted almost half of Jewell's doubts. Any remaining objections in Jewell's mind were swept away when she learned that Mrs. Croft was a member of the Daughters of the American Revolution, the American Association of University Women, and the Genealogy Group of Washtenaw County in the Lower Peninsula. The little boys from the Detroit Baptist Mission would be a group of ten only, and would be chosen for their gentlemanly manners and quiet demeanor.

Ann, who was taking her tea near the fireplace away from the oak table, smiled in amusement as the remaining listed restrictions were crossed off, one by one, under the charm of the Admiral and his wife. Even the library was to remain open for afternoon tea, under the stipulation of course, that the books were not to be handled or read.

After the remaining terms were agreed upon and the future renters were preparing to leave, Mrs. Croft came toward the fireplace and remarked to Ann that one of her brothers would be staying with them for a visit also. "Perhaps you have heard the name

Wentworth? My younger brother worked on the Island one summer a few years ago. That is where he learned of Huntingdon Lodge and persuaded us to visit the area. We are grateful to him for that."

Ann's hand began to shake as she set her teacup down. She was about to reply when Jewell, who had been on the far side of the table and had not heard Mrs. Croft's inquiry, came around to her with a smile and her concluding greetings.

Ann's heart was still fluttering as she realized that the sight of the phantom runner had perhaps not been an illusion after all and that she would once again see Frederick Wentworth. As she went up the stairs to her room, she was all amazement. Who would have thought, she marveled, that he could perhaps soon be watching the summer moonrise from her very window!

And Jewell had her own disturbing thoughts to consider. She was marveling that she was not only deigning to rent her home, but actually leaving her Woodleigh Hall to the occupancy of a "mixed" couple. For Mrs. Croft was as pale skinned as her husband was dark. What would Nettie have said? She was glad that she would never hear her sister make a snide comment on Jewell's lowering herself to such a demeaning transaction. As she entered the great hall to give Serle the instructions for dinner, she imagined Nettie speaking from her grave, saying, "What is this world coming to!"

Chapter VI

The work of clearing and organizing Nettie's mansion cottage on the Island now must give way to the clearing of Woodleigh Hall to make ready for the new occupants.

Ann could make short work of her own organizing, having been away at school and of necessity knowing what part of her wardrobe must be sent to the Island for the summer and which could be stored in the Hall. She boxed her favorite books in order to clear the shelves in her room, wondering which guests may be staying there. The room looked so bare without books that she at first arranged six Jane Austen and six mystery books at either end of the top shelf and stood back to admire the balanced look. But then deciding that she must take her current Austen that she was re-reading, and not wanting to leave an incomplete set in either house, packed all the Austen and left one book of British mysteries and a King James Bible to balance the shelf.

The top desk drawer, however, was a more difficult sorting job with its tiny scraps of memorabilia. She was tilting the removed drawer over the wastebasket when she stopped to scoop the larger bits into her hand. At once, the touch of a tiny scrap of mottled stone caused her to pause and finger it carefully. She was immediately sent back into a summer day on the shore of the Island where it had been found.

She recalled Frederick's saying, "Let's quit this beachcombing and go for some fudge and coffee."

"Not until we get a take-home. Remember the rules; nothing that won't fit into a teaspoon," Ann replied.

"Then here it is. Look I found a Petoskey! It's too big, but I can break it apart." And he handed her a tiny chip of the fossilized rock.

Now as she gazed at it, the warmth of the memory overcame the value of the rock specimen. It was considered lucky to find a piece of the state stone of Michigan, but this tiny fragment was not large enough to save as a display nor perfect enough to mount as a piece of jewelry. Then remembering a photo locket from her jewel box that was rather dented and missing a chain, she decided it could be a place to save the stone, and to keep it from being assigned to the junk pile. The inside of the photo locket proved to be just large enough to contain it. She snapped it shut and placed it back into her jewel box.

As she descended to the drawing room, she could hear Jewell addressing Henry in a decisive tone. "I hope you can get rid of these electric tricks and gadgets around the house. We certainly don't need that silly recorded laugh greeting visitors at the front door."

Henry left to do her bidding, and in the drawing room Jewell continued directing Serle with nervous gestures in matters of packing and moving boxes, while Elizabeth ordered Penny about with languid waves of the hand as she leaned against the grand piano.

Jewell had another, albeit unspoken, reason favoring a move to the Island; she was hoping that Elizabeth would leave Penny Clay behind and bestow more affection on and attention to her sister Ann, whom Jewell thought more deserving than the divorced friend from a distinctly lower class.

When Elizabeth saw Ann, she seemed gratified to have another person to direct. Ann was allowed no opinions or decisions in the storing of any articles. This was usually the case. Ann's opinion never mattered. She was only Ann, the youngest sister, and her opinions were of little consequence among the others.

Jewell's plan for displacing Penny was thwarted when Mary telephoned from Upper-cross asking Ann to come stay with her. Mary was ill, and Mrs. Miggs, her live-in baby sitter and general maid, would soon be leaving for a visit to her own family. Because Mary was so sensitive and seemed to imagine catching every virus blowing across the Straits, it was impossible to determine how ill Mary really was, but Ann was glad for a change of scene, happy to feel needed, and looked forward to seeing Mary and Charles' little boys who declared Ann was their favorite aunt.

And Elizabeth immediately repeated her invitation. "As Ann will be staying at Upper-cross, you must take the lower tower room at the Island cottage, Penny. There will be plenty of room." Jewell could think of no proper objection, and the arrangement seemed to be settled.

The cottage gatehouse for Huntingdon Lodge stood at the upper crossing of Rushy Creek on the main road to Rushy Falls. Formerly boasting a post office and general store, the settlement had diminished to a single dwelling, and the name had shrunk to Uppercross, but the stone cottage itself had expanded with additions of brick and timber to a spreading two-story house, without outgrowing the appellation of cottage. The iron gateway gracing the stone wall stood permanently open, and only the little stone sentry house beside it, which was now Trapper's dog house, indicated that the cottage had been the gatehouse for the great house, Huntingdon Lodge, farther down the lane. Mary and Charles with their two children lived in the Uppercross cottage and kept in close communication with the Lodge where Charles' parents and his two sisters lived. The elder Mr. and Mrs. Musgrove operated their Lodge as a small hotel, and Charles was the principal guide for the hunters and tourists.

On the May afternoon when Ann arrived at Uppercross Cottage, she found Mary propped in her big bed, her brown curls fluffed out against the lace edged pillow. On her knees was a crossword puzzle book, and nearby were a box of chocolates and a package of cough drops. As Ann entered, Mary reached for a tissue from the bedside stand, blew her nose daintily, and declared, "I thought you'd never come. I've been so down with this terrible cold. Charles makes light of all my ailments. I can never convince him I am ill, and the little boys have been just wild. Mrs. Miggs cannot keep them from running in here at all hours, and I cannot get a bit of rest. Could you bring me a glass of water? Maybe if I take another cold tablet I'll be able to get up for a little while."

Ann apologized for her delay in coming and began to explain the arrangements that were going on at Woodleigh Hall, but Mary was interested only in relating details of her own situation. "No one at the Lodge has called or expressed any concern over my illness. You would think Henrietta or Louisa at least would have phoned."

As if in answer to her complaint, Mrs. Miggs came in to announce that Louisa and Henrietta Musgrove had arrived to inquire about Mary.

"I'll come down for a few minutes. Ann, hand me my slippers. Maybe a little sociability will do me good." The combination of Ann and the new callers proved to be the needed cure. With tea and conversation Mary's strength improved so rapidly that she began to declare her intention to walk out with the Musgrove sisters to accompany them back to the Lodge.

Henrietta, the elder sister, about Ann's age, dressed in a wool plaid walking skirt and jacket, sat quietly while her younger sister chattered rapidly. Louisa, about seventeen, wearing jeans and a yellow shirt was a veritable butterfly with her pretty face, blond hair, and youthful energy. Her conversation flitted from topic to topic in non-stop delivery.

"Charles is always tying up the phone with his computer, and we can never make our own calls. Papa says we're getting another line but the phone company must have us on the bottom of the list for the whole U.P. So we decided to come in person to see how Mary is. We're glad you're here, Ann. It's been so dull lately. No guests yet at the Lodge, and we can't have a decent Saturday dance party with so few people. I have new western boots to go with my blue full skirt, and I haven't even broken them in yet. But we're hoping everything will be better next week. Charles says Admiral Croft is coming back and bringing his wife, her married brother and two children. I wish Henrietta's boyfriend was home from seminary. He doesn't approve of couple dancing, but maybe he will go along with our line and square dances, and we'll at least have enough pairs to try the contra dances Mama likes to play."

Married brother? Henrietta chattered on toward other topics, but Ann felt as if a door had slammed in her face. No one noticed her suddenly pale face and sharp intake of breath. Frederick married? Of course he could be. Why shouldn't he be?

Ann was grateful that no one here knew of her great disappointment. None knew how special Ann's friendship with the young carriage driver had been. During that summer, Elizabeth was away at modeling school, Mary was lying in with her first child, and the Musgrove sisters came to the Island only when they had visiting friends or relatives who wanted to see the Fort and the Grand Hotel.

The four young women started out on the short walk to the Lodge. For Ann the muddy road was not as much a hindrance to walking as was the heaviness of her heart.

Chapter VII

The final week of May had come, and the Von Russetts had left for the house on Big Turtle Island, the Crofts had arrived at Woodleigh Hall, and Ann remained at Uppercross. Mary had quite recovered, but because Mrs. Miggs had not yet returned, Ann was prevailed upon to stay at Uppercross a little longer. Ann's agreement was perhaps due not only to the pleasant hospitality of Mary, Charles, and their little boys, but also to the entertaining company of the Musgrove sisters and the prospect of the dance party planned for the near future. And even though the knowledge that Frederick was married and would be bringing his wife and family to Woodleigh where Ann would certainly meet them soon, her curiosity haunted her thoughts like a painful tooth.

It was rumored that the Crofts would be arriving with a large party of friends and relatives, among them three men on leave from the Coast Guard. The rain which had kept the roads nearly impassable between Woodleigh and Uppercross finally ceased, and bright sunshine arrived with scudding clouds which seemed to wash the sky clean and warm the earth with the promise of a glorious summer.

One morning Ann was supervising the little boys at a table full of blocks and crayons when Louisa ran in almost breathless with the latest news.

"The Crofts are moving in! But our information is all wrong. There are only two sailors. And both of Mrs. Croft's brothers will be here, the married one and the sailor who is in the Coast Guard. Charles said he met him this spring when he was in St Ambrose. He's supposed to be tall and handsome."

"What is his name?" inquired Ann.

"I don't know. But I hope he likes to dance." And on that note Luisa ran upstairs to find Mary and repeat the news.

The following day Ann and Mary were finishing their breakfast in the little trellised room at the rear of Uppercross Cottage. It was the first morning warm enough to use the veranda, which was open on one side, letting in the sunshine and still brisk air. Mary, who was facing the path toward the Lodge announced, "Here comes Charles and someone else running with the dog."

Ann's view was from the other side of the table, and not wanting to display an overly eager curiosity, picked up her coffee cup and sat back to wait for her own view of the runners.

Charles and his companion soon appeared at the edge of the porch, pausing only long enough for Charles to say, "Mary, meet Frederick Wentworth." and turning to address Frederick, added, "My wife's sister, Ann."

Trapper tugged at the leash and lunged ahead, eager to be off again. Frederick gave only the merest glance toward Ann and uttered a quick "Hi." Their eyes met.

Ann replied with the same greeting and was trying unsuccessfully to add some additional comments when Frederick turned and ran down the lane to follow Charles and the dog.

"Well, that was quick," Mary remarked. "Their morning jog is more important than being sociable. You'd think they could at least ask us to join them. Of course, with my knees, Charles knows I don't run, but what do you think of the new guest?"

Ann concealed her flustered reaction by pretending to choke on her last swallow of coffee and then pushed her cup forward, asking for a refill. She was almost grateful that she had had no time to say anything to the runners because she had been truly at a loss for words.

Regaining her composure, she said, "He looks familiar. I think he may have been one of the carriage drivers on the Island the summer I worked there."

Mary continued talking about the general discourtesy of most men, the thoughtless behavior of her husband in particular, and the problems of raising two little boys with a father as indulgent as Charles.

Ann nodded, simulating an attentive conversationalist while trying to recover from her amazement. Here he was-Frederick Wentworth, more mature, more handsome, and still able to stop her breath. But her happiness in seeing him was crushed with the overpowering realization that he had not even recognized her.

The Crofts were now settled in Woodleigh Hall and the Musgroves were eager to welcome them to the neighborhood. The Crofts accepted with alacrity an invitation to dine at Huntingdon Lodge on the following Friday, and the plan caused a great deal of interest at the Cottage. Charles talked of joining the dinner party, but Mary had objections.

"Charles, you forget that Mrs. Miggs is not here to watch the children. You think you can gad off anytime you please. I'm just as eager to meet the Crofts as you are, but you know the evening will last too late to take the boys."

Ann decided to make the noble gesture of offering to stay at the cottage with the boys so that both Mary and Charles could go. "I've already met the Crofts, and I'm sure we'll all get together again before they leave. Let me stay here with the children this time."

Their faint protests were overcome by Ann's repetition of the offer, and Ann was left to a quiet evening, remaining in suspense a little longer over the question regarding which of Mrs. Croft's brothers was the married one.

The dinner party was a great success. Charles' sisters arrived at the Cottage the following morning with all the gossip that Ann wanted. Louisa bubbled excitedly with her news.

"Mrs. Croft is ever so charming, and her husband is so clever. Her married brother and family have not arrived, and instead Frederick brought his friend Ben. Ben is very quiet and kind of gloomy, but, Ann, you should go over to the Hall and see Frederick. He thinks he knows you. He asked if you had ever worked on Turtle Island. He said you must've cut your hair and looked so much older than when he knew you. He is so handsome. He was telling us all about the Coast Guard. We're all invited to Woodleigh Hall for dinner next Wednesday. And Frederick does like to dance! We are persuading Papa to have a party next Saturday. There will be a bus load of tourists at the Lodge for the weekend, and we can ask Mr. Rundull to play the violin."

Even Henrietta was thrilled at the prospect of dancing with Frederick. The conversation gravitated to which sister would wear the fringed skirt. They shared their clothes and traded so often it became a major confab as to who would wear what and which blouses matched which slacks or skirts.

So he had remembered her after all! Was his extra brief greeting on the veranda that morning due to doubt on his part, to embarrassed shyness, or only to a cool indifference? Yes, her hair used to be long instead of the short boy-cap of curls she now wore, but "so much older"? That sounded horrible!

Ann was specifically included in the invitation to dine at the Hall, and as Mrs. Miggs was due back on Monday, they would all be free to attend.

The weather turned cold again on Monday, and Mrs. Miggs arrived as scheduled. Then the wind rose with a drenching rain that threatened to mire the road between the Cottage and Woodleigh Hall. But Wednesday dawned bright and sparkling. Charles left early in the afternoon in compliance with a request from his sisters. They thought it would be fun to take Frederick for a ride in the cart before dinner and insisted that Charles hitch up the horse and drive them over to the Hall. Ann and Mary followed later in the car.

How strange it will be, thought Ann, to be in her own home, but with strangers as hosts. She wondered which room Frederick was staying in and if it was her own, whether or not he recognized any of her possessions there.

The Crofts welcomed them at the door and led them to the great hall which was livened with a fire on the hearth and country music playing from the library. The long table was set with the earthenware breakfast dishes instead of Jewell's fine china, but little candles in wooden holders at intervals along the table furnished a homey yet festive air.

"Well, you see, Ann, we're not so fine as your aunt, but we enjoy the house in our own way, and have managed to settle in," said the Admiral. "Though we do rattle around in this big place. Mrs. Croft needs a ship's horn to summon me because I get lost so far away in those upper rooms. I'm glad there is a bell for dinner. I haven't missed any meals yet."

Mrs. Croft added her greetings and her appreciation to the Von Russets for retaining Serle to manage the house. "I am thoroughly enjoying being spoiled with all the help," she said, leading them to chairs by the fire where Mr. and Mrs. Musgrove were warming themselves along with a pale young man with high forehead and pointed chin.

The pale young man was introduced as Captain Benjamin Benwick, a friend of Frederick, visiting from Tawas City. He was recovering from a bad cold, he said, and so had the perfect excuse for not going out in the cart. In taking Ann's coat, Mrs. Croft whispered,

"He is having a hard time recovering from the loss of his wife. You can cheer him up, Ann."

The conversation kept them from remarking on the lateness of the hour. Serle came in to ask about keeping the meat warm, when they heard the rest of the company arrive. They stomped in noisily with apologies for being late, but looked as if they were enjoying themselves immensely. Henrietta and Louisa were laughing and blaming Charles for their delay. "He drove so fast we nearly tipped out of the cart! And then he said the horse was too tired to pull us up the slope and we had to get out and walk. Look at the mud on our shoes!"

Henrietta had escaped with only smudges, but Louisa's feet were soaked. Frederick seated her close to the fire, helped her take her shoes off, and rubbed her cold feet as she held them toward the flames. Mrs. Croft fetched some slippers for her to wear, and dinner was announced.

The Admiral sat at the head of the table,

which had been shortened to accommodate the ten diners, with Mrs. Croft on his left. There was no formal arrangement for seating and the Musgrove girls took seats nearer the fire, expecting Frederick to join them, but Ann found herself next to Frederick at the foot of the table. He began with,

"Well, it's been awhile. I think we actually are old friends."

"Acquaintances, at least," replied Ann coolly. And because the rest of the conversation circled within the entire group, there were no more personal exchanges between the former sweethearts until near the end of the evening.

Henrietta and Louisa were charmed by the handsome Frederick, and he basked in the glow of their attention. They asked questions about the Coast Guard and listened with rapt attention as he related tales of his training and some of the rescue missions on the Great Lakes.

Mr. Musgrove expressed an interest in lighthouses. "Aren't you fellows the ones who keep the lighthouses lit?"

"All of the lights are automated now," put in Captain Benwick. "And many of the old lighthouses have been turned into museums after being decommissioned. But there's one light that refuses to go dark."

"What do you mean?"

"Old Bleak Point Light is maintained by a ghost. Frederick has seen it himself." In answer to excited queries Frederick told the story.

"A new automated light was put up at Bleak Point closer to the shore, and the old light was to be decommissioned. But Abner Davis, the elderly keeper, refused to leave. The townspeople of Bixby rallied behind him and voted to turn the tower and adjoining house into a museum with Davis as the docent. Everyone realized his health was poor. The Fresnel lens was removed, the electricity was turned off in the tower, and Abner Davis died soon after that. His wife continued living there as hostess and docent, but one night on her way home she saw a light in the tower. When she investigated, she found nothing there.

"Then the authorities called and told her not to put a light in the tower because it would be confusing to ships taking readings from the new light which was situated farther out on the point. She swore she was not putting a light there and assisted them in an investigation which turned up nothing. She declared it was the spirit of Abner putting a light in the tower for her return home.

"Mrs. Davis has been dead several years, but people still see the glow from the tower on moonless nights. Even passing ships have reported it."

Charles objected, "Couldn't someone be putting a lantern up there to keep the story alive?"

"The Coast Guard authorities investigated with the help of the State Police, but all the theories—reflections, teenage pranksters, moonlight, swamp gas, were all disproved. I've seen the light myself from the Badger, the carferry out of Ludington."

"Where does the ferry go from Ludington?"

"To Manitowoc, Wisconsin. I know the captain and have crossed with him several times."

Louisa showed an immediate interest in traveling on the ferry in order to see the ghost light, but the conversation moved on to steamships, mysterious islands and historic storms.

Mrs. Musgrove was probably the heartiest in her praise of Frederick Wentworth and his duties. She was ready to give immediate approval to anyone in the Coast Guard as a consequence of her son Richard having been saved after a boating accident off North Manitou Island two years before. Richard was a devil-may-care wastrel who ran with a rowdy gang of friends, and his sisters had confided to Ann that his accident was due to an excess of alcohol in an overcrowded boat, but Mrs. Musgrove so doted on her boy that she always emphasized the size of the waves, and the mechanical failure of the engines whenever she told of the event. She proceeded to do so now with great detail.

And where was Richard now? He had dropped out of college and had gone to bicycle around Europe. No message had come from him in over a year. But Mrs. Musgrove was sure he must have gone to sea, "Because he loved the water so" and she gazed at Frederick as if grateful to him for being a part of that branch of service that locates and saves everyone lost at sea.

After her detailed account of Richard's escapade, she turned to Frederick and asked, "Surely, you've heard of him? He's very well known in boating circles."

As she turned away to wipe her eyes, Ann caught Frederick's eye and smiled at the absurdity of the comments. Frederick suppressed a grin, and as he covered his mouth to give a slight cough, returned Ann's glance with a wink.

It was only a glance, but with that look, Ann's heart was warmed. It was as if all their old friendship and similar feeling rushed back with its former strength and the five years between their former acquaintance were as nothing.

Then his look hardened and his attention turned back to the group, finally softening with the smiles and questions from the Musgrove sisters. The evening ended with plans for the forthcoming party at the Lodge, and as they rose from the table, Frederick hastened to escort them to the car, but there were no special words of farewell for Ann.

Chapter VIII

Frederick Wentworth was now the most popular newcomer to the neighborhood. He met only warm admiration from everyone, but Henrietta and and Louisa especially seemed entirely occupied by him. Only the fact that the sisters had always had perfect good will for each other prevented them from being seen as rivals. It was soon Huntingdon Lodge for Frederick every day, and he became the focus of the talk at the Cottage.

"Which of your sisters do you think he prefers, Charles?" asked Mary.

Charles was putting on his coat to go out, but he paused at the door to give his opinion. "Louisa seems to be the most active in pursuit," he replied, "but Henrietta is more attractive. Have you noticed how Louisa calls him Ricky? Where did she get that name for him?"

"He said he hates having his name shortened to Fred, so she took the 'rick' part and calls him Ricky."

Ann remembered that Frederick never used to want his name shortened at all. What indulgence a man will allow under the influence of a little charmer!

Mary persisted, "Wasn't Henrietta supposed to be engaged to Adam Hayter?"

"There wasn't any formal commitment."

"I think Frederick would be a better match for her. Adam is so strict in his beliefs—no dancing, no short hair. I know Henrietta is more sedate than Louisa, but I'd hate to see her tied down to Adam."

"He's not all that bad. And the family has plenty of money. His family turned down his scholarship at the Bible college he enrolled in and donated the tuition." Charles seemed to think his comment ended the discussion, and he left the room.

"But Ann," Mary asked, "Why didn't you set your cap for him yourself?"

"I guess I don't have a cap to set," laughed Ann.

But secretly she wondered how Frederick really felt. Was he aware of the danger in encouraging the affections of two people at once? Was he flaunting his popularity to impress a former flame? She recalled the one knowing glance they had shared at the dinner party, but on all occasions since then he had remained only coldly polite.

The plans for the dance party proceeded smoothly. Charles sent an e-mail invitation to the Von Russetts on Turtle Island, but Henry sent regrets for himself and the others. Turtle Island was only half an hour by ferryboat from the Peninsula, but it was a world unto itself, and the Von Russetts were totally involved in their own social circle.

Neighbor Mr. Rundull agreed to furnish violin music and arrived early on the designated day in order to practice the chosen numbers with Mrs. Musgrove at the piano.

The hall at Huntingdon Lodge was originally a garage for snowmobiles, a rough addition to the main edifice which contained several well-furnished guest rooms in addition to the family living quarters. But the hall made up in size what it lacked in elegance, and with little red lanterns at intervals and benches along the walls, it became quite a suitable ballroom.

Upstairs Henrietta and Louisa were assembling their party clothes. Louisa decided that her new boots went well with the blue full skirt, but Henrietta decided to wear green slacks that covered the tops of her Peter Pan shoes. She unpinned her braids and let down her chestnut hair which fell in waves to her waist. When Ann saw her, she admitted to herself that Henrietta was alluring, but wondered if her lipstick wasn't a little too dark, and her slacks a little too snug to be attractive. She hoped her own red dress would set the proper tone and qualify her as an attractive dance partner.

Because Ann, Mary, and Charles were the first to arrive, Mrs. Musgrove gave them orders to help.

"Mary, go help in the kitchen. The punch needs mixing. Charles, you can get more ice from the freezer. Ann, you'll have to help me hold the music on this rickety rack and turn the pages as I play. "

The new electric piano funished enough volume, but the music rack was too short and the stool rather small for a person of Mrs. Musgrove's considerable bulk. She quite hung over the edges as she sat on it, and Ann hoped it was sturdy enough to hold her weight for the entire evening.

Henrietta and Louisa entered just as the promised busload of tourists arrived. Mr. Musgrove welcomed them with his booming voice and hearty laugh.

"Put your coats on the hooks, your hats on the rack, and your feet on the floor. No sitting down till after the first set. You've been riding too long and need to stretch out."

Mr. Rundull pulled his bow across the violin, Mrs. Musgrove struck a loud chord, and as Mr. Musgrove called the directions, everyone formed a big circle, and the dance began. The big circle became smaller ones, pairs were counted off, the rhythm quickened, and the merriment increased. At the end of the set everyone was laughing and some were quite out of breath.

Just as the music resumed for the next number Admiral and Mrs. Croft, along with Frederick and Captain Benwick, entered the hall. Louisa ran forward to greet Frederick, and Henrietta took possession of the Captain, steering him toward a vacant space in the circle. Mr. Musgrove's smooth instructions and risible comments led even the inexperienced dancers easily into the more complicated figures.

"Big foot up and little foot down
Like a chicken walkin' on frozen ground
Corn's in the crib and wheat's in the stack
Meet your honey and turn right back."

Ann felt doomed to stand forever as page turner with no chance to dance, until she noticed a teen-aged boy in a baggy red sweatshirt sitting on a nearby bench and during the next break asked him if he'd like to help turn pages. Mrs. Musgrove heard her request and said, "This next one's a schottische; I don't need to read the music for this one. Go ahead and dance."

So Ann and the young man joined the other couples. The young man was rather reluctant to try an unfamiliar dance, but he cooperated from a sense of duty, thinking he could perhaps earn the position of page turner later on.

"One-two-three-hop, One-two-three-hop
"Step-hop, step-hop, step-hop, step-hop.

He caught on quickly, in spite of his too-long sleeves getting in the way as they turned, but his rhythm was fine and he found entertainment in swinging Ann around as fast as he could. They soon became the head of the line as other couples watched and then imitated the steps behind them. Ann noticed Frederick watching her and wondered if he still thought her "so much older."

When the number ended she found herself standing next to Captain Benwick. He bowed formally and asked her for the next dance. It was a waltz and he was adept with the steps and smooth with the turns as he led her around the floor.

She was beginning to despair of ever having a chance to dance with Frederick, when she saw him look at her and head toward her during the pause between numbers. But before he reached her, the red sweatshirt boy asked her to show him how to polka, and she accepted the challenge. The music reached a furious pace and all the dancers were trying to keep up. Everyone became overheated with the effort and the big garage-size door at the end of the hall was opened at the conclusion of the number to let in the cool air.

A visitor, arriving late and seeing the big open door decided to enter there, but as he stepped into the room, he was stopped by the spectacle before him. The late arrival was none other than Adam Hayter, home from seminary and coming to call on his sweetheart Henrietta. But what he saw left him dismayed and frozen in horror. For there she was standing very close to a strange man who had his arm around her waist. Her long hair was no longer in its neat wreath of braids, but flowing freely around her shoulders as she looked up smiling at her partner. Ann saw that the angle of his view could not be less shocking because Henrietta's back was to the door presenting to view her attractive derriere in the too-snug slacks.

Henrietta, noticing that Frederick was looking at someone over her shoulder, turned and gasped as she saw Adam. She started toward him, but Adam had seen enough. He strode back out into the night, and before Henrietta could reach him, got into his car and drove away.

By the time Henrietta returned to the dance floor, Louisa had appropriated Frederick and the next dance began. This time it was an old English contra-dance, and Mr. Musgrove insisted that everyone take part. Henrietta claimed Captain Benwick, and because Mary had left to check on the children who were asleep upstairs, Charles invited Ann into the circle. Mr. Musgrove began by "stirring the pot"—insisting that each gentleman move to the left and take a new lady as partner. For Frederick it was Ann. She was actually going to dance with him! The pattern proved to be more walking than dancing, and its slow and stately measures allowed intervals for conversation.

Mr. Musgrove began by asking the two lines to approach and bow to partners, then return to place. As they advanced toward each other, Frederick began,

"What have you been doing these past few years?"
"Among other things, waiting for your letter."

Mr. Musgrove boomed the next instruction to approach again with a right arm turn.

.

"I wrote to you," Frederick said.
"I never received it," she answered.

Forward again with a left arm turn.
"I had proof that you did."

"What proof?"

"Long gone." This last phrase was spoken with a downward inflection and a distinct formality. His tone of indifference implied that any previous relationship was also beyond recovery.

The next call sent them separately down the line of dancers, pairing everyone with different partners and making impossible any further conversation.

The party ended with a buffet supper. Captain Benwick led Ann to the dining room and she tried to make pleasant small talk. But she had appetite only for the mystery of the missing letter.

Chapter IX

F rederick Wentworth and Captain Benwick
were scheduled to leave soon, and Ann
was despairing of having further opportunity
to talk with Frederick. Then Henrietta
announced her intention of showing the men
the Tahassee Falls before they left.

The falls of the Upper Tahassee were a
great tourist attraction during the summer
season and with the recent spring rains would
be at their roaring best. But the drive there
and return would take the greater part of a
day. Louisa, more in favor of a hike than a
drive, suggested they visit the Lower Tahassee Falls instead. The hike there would be
only a half day walk along a gravel road.

Mary and Charles approved the plan, and
the following morning after packing sand-
wiches and water bottles in the knapsacks,
the seven started out. Louisa again amended
the plan.

"This road is too straight and boring. Let's go by way of the trail. It's not much longer and we'll see wildflowers that way."

No objections were made, and the group started out through the forest. The path was wide at first and the hikers could walk several abreast, but as it narrowed, only two could walk together at a time. Louisa and Henrietta were both vying for positions next to Frederick. The conversation was lively and the couples were shuffled and positions changed as someone spotted a jack-in-the-pulpit or a yellow mallow and called attention to it. Trapper bounced alongside merrily, investigating smells along the path and seeking affection from each couple as she ran back and forth.

Captain Benwick often trailed behind in order to photograph an especially interesting scene, and the group moved more slowly. Ann decided to run ahead to the knoll, a favorite spot above the trail which was shaded by trees on the east side but gave a beautiful view of wooded hills to the west. She stopped there to admire the view and suddenly realized the main trail passed immediately below her, although concealed from her view, because she could hear conversation. She was about to call to them to climb up when she heard Louisa say to Frederick,

"I wish Charles had married Ann instead of Mary. He wanted to date her first, you know."

"Really?" Frederick seemed very interested.

"She went out with him once, but I think it was her Aunt Jewell who discouraged the whole thing. She didn't think Charles was educated enough, or something. The Von Russetts are very proud. They think themselves of a higher class than we are."

"Is that so?"

"Jewell was always very strict with the Eliot sisters, but Mary has a mind of her own. I think I am like that. I would never be so easily persuaded to drop someone I like."

"I admire you for that," he replied. "It's good to have a mind of your own and to stand firm for what you want."

Ann was afraid to move for fear of being seen, and quite full of emotion at what she had heard. As Mary and Charles came by, she climbed back down to the main trail and joined Benwick who was walking in the rear.

Mary began to complain that they'd never get to the falls unless they hurried up, and her objections grew even stronger when Charles suggested that they stop to see the Hayters. Their route led within a quarter mile of the Hayter homestead down a steep side path.

"Forget about the Hayters. Adam thinks he's too good for us, anyway. You saw how he walked out of the hall at the party. Henrietta doesn't care about him anymore, and I'd say she's well rid of him."

But Charles replied, "You don't need to come down. You can take a break here and we'll be back pretty soon. I'd like to show Frederick and Ben the little log chapel. They haven't seen it yet."

Captain Benwick declined in favor of staying with the others at the top of the hill, but Frederick and Charles started down the path.

Ann was glad of the rest. Usually a good hiker, she had chosen her heavier new boots instead of her running shoes, and her left heel was now threatening to become rubbed into a blister. She found herself sitting next to Benwick on a log as she removed her boot and smoothed out a wrinkle in her sock.

"Isn't this a great time of year?" she asked him. "The only thing better than spring is summer."

"A love of Nature is supposed to cheer us up. I guess. 'She creeps into our saddest moments with a mild and healing sympathy.'"

"That's a line from 'Thanatopsis,' isn't it? Such a gloomy poem. I hated it in school, and we had to memorize the ending—all about approaching our grave wearing drapes or something."

Then she recalled Mrs. Croft's whispered comment that Captain Benwick was in mourning and Ann had been asked to help.

"I'm sorry about the loss of your wife. When did she pass away?"

"She didn't die. She ran off with another man"

"Oh, I'm sorry. You had no warning?"

"None at all. And I have no idea where she is. So I guess it's like a death. A whole year has gone by and I still think about it."

"But how do you know she is still with him? Haven't you tried to trace her?"

"I'm not sure if I should. I don't know if I want to."

Ann finished tying her boot. "But you should not dwell on it. You've got to get out of the death-poetry mode. I know some good reading for you—pop psychology titles and some funny novels I can recommend."

Ann smiled at the irony of her situation—giving advice to another about forgetting an old love, while she herself had not been very successful in that regard.

The conversation was interrupted by the approach of Frederick and Charles coming up the hill with a third person who turned out to be Adam Hayter. Cordial greetings were exchanged and Adam agreed to join them on the walk to the falls.

The group set off again. As the path widened enough for couples, Henrietta was paired with Adam. They lagged behind the others and became involved in their own conversation.

Ann mused on the success of Louisa's maneuverings. Had she purposely led the group toward the Hayter farm in hopes of a meeting between Henrietta and Adam? If they reconciled, Louisa would have eliminated a rival in her pursuit of Frederick.

Just before the falls, the path joined the road, and as they approached it, there came Admiral and Mrs. Croft in the little pony cart. There had evidently been some good natured bantering going on, and Mrs. Croft was laughing and telling the Admiral to stop his teasing.

"Hello!" she called. "The falls are beautiful. Quite a roaring. The Admiral tells me if I'd quit talking I could actually hear them! I guess I need someone to help keep him in line. Does anyone want a ride back to Uppercross with us?"

Frederick stepped forward and spoke to the Crofts, then turned to Ann. "Wouldn't you like a ride back? I noticed you're limping."

Ann accepted gratefully. She had seen the falls many times, and by avoiding the return walk she could perhaps fend off the incipient blister.

The offer caught her by surprise. Surprise that Frederick had noticed her discomfort and surprise that this little kindness singled her out in a thoughtful way.

Her hopes rose at the idea, then fell again as she saw Louisa take his arm and say, "Come on, Ricky. They're way ahead of us already."

He took Louisa's arm and continued with the others along the path. Ann climbed into the cart and tried to contribute to the bantering conversation of the Crofts as they rode back to Uppercross.

Chapter X

Frederick and Ben were dinner guests at Uppercross Cottage the following evening when the subject of lighthouses came up again. Frederick and Ben had just one week left to enjoy the company of the Uppercross circle, but Louisa was still wild to visit lighthouses and have the men show her the haunted ones they had talked of. Mary left the table to tend to the children and Louisa began insisting they plan an excursion.

Captain Benwick suggested they take a trip along the eastern shore of the Lower Peninsula and see the lights along Lake Huron. He said that the Old Presque Isle Lighthouse was more famous than the one near Ludington. Frederick added that if they went as far as the Tawases they could visit Forty Mile Point as well as Presque Isle and the light at Tawas Point. Besides, he knew some of the men at the Tawas Coast Guard

Station and would like to introduce his friends there. If they went directly to Tawas, the trip would take only one day.

Louisa was enthusiastic about seeing East Tawas and the piers. Henrietta was all for pier walking. She would love to see the yachts moored there. Ann remembered that Tawas, on Lake Huron, was billed as "The Sunrise Side" of Michigan; she had not seen nearby Iargo Springs and the long stairway down to the Au Sable River there. Mention of the AuSable brought the conversation to the Canoe Marathon and questions about when that event would take place. As the sightseeing plan began to expand, they realized that in order to see all the lights, and have enough time to climb the towers and watch for a ghost light after dark, they would need two days or more for the trip.

That plan was gaining general approval and details of the preparation were being laid out when Mary returned and voiced a strong objection to the plan. They asked why.

Her answer plainly and simply was one word—the Bridge. The five-mile Mighty Mack Bridge spanned the Straits of Mackinac, connecting Michigan's Upper and

Lower Peninsulas since 1958. The beautiful suspension, the longest in the country, rose hundreds of feet above the waters where Lake Michigan on the west and Lake Huron on the east came together. For most people it served as a scenic interlude on the way to the Soo Locks and Canada. But for Mary, and for anyone with acrophobia, it was a fearful barrier. The Bridge was Mary's *bete noir*. She would go to any lengths to avoid using it. Many times she had taken the ferry to Turtle Island from St. Ambrose in the Upper Peninsula and another ferry from there to Mackinaw City to reach the south side. And Charles was no help. He ridiculed her phobia and had on occasion tried to force her to face it directly in the manner of throwing a person into the water in order to teach him to swim.

"You can just stay at home," he said. "It's ridiculous to make us wait for you at Mackinaw City while you do the double boat ride. going and coming."

"I'm not being ridiculous! You know there are even truck drivers who get someone else to drive across for them."

Louisa chimed in, "But they are still in their rigs; they're just not driving. You can sit in back between Ann and me and keep your eyes closed."

Frederick intervened in what he saw could become an impasse. "Could you bear to cross just once? If we went to the west shore to see Ludington instead of Tawas, we could cross Lake Michigan on the Badger Car Ferry, drive north through Wisconsin and complete a circle back to Uppercross without re-crossing the bridge.

Mary's desire to be included finally overcame her objections and she agreed to be a part of the group on the circle trip to Ludington.

The next day as room reservations were being made, there came an obstacle from another quarter—Turtle Island. On being invited to join them, Elizabeth and Penny had declined, already caught up in their social obligations on the Island. But Aunt Jewell objected to the excursion itself as unsafe and improper. She reminded them that the chosen weekend would be one of heavy tourist traffic, making driving dangerous. In addition, the young people should not be going on overnight trips unchaperoned.

Ann explained that except for the bridge, they'd be avoiding major highways, that

Mary and Charles, as a married couple, would be quite suitable as chaperons, and that the young women would have their own hotel rooms apart from the men.

Although Ann's explanation seemed to quiet her objection on those two counts, Jewell asked that at least Ann move to the Island instead of taking the trip, her reason being that they had heard from the long-lost distant cousin William Eliot. He was actually on his way to visit them on Turtle Island and was bringing a friend. Ann should be on the Island to meet them and help show them around.

Ann realized that Jewell's main goals were to see her nieces comfortably married, and to see the Eliot name continue. Jewell also believed that the expected Mr. Eliot and his friend would be of a more acceptable social class than that of the Uppercross crowd, and although she did not voice this last opinion openly, Ann understood that idea as being the main force behind the urgency of the invitation.

Ann promised to join Jewell and the rest of the family the following week, but as she had already promised to be a part of the Ludington excursion, she would not disappoint the others by canceling her reservation. Jewell grudgingly accepted her decision, and planning for the trip proceeded.

Ben mentioned the bed-and-breakfast inn of the Harvilles, a family he and Frederick had known at Ludington when their son was in the Coast Guard, but as they planned to take the night boat in order to see the haunted lighthouse, they would not be planning to stay overnight in Ludington.

The excitement mounted rapidly. Maps were studied, suitcases were packed, and the weather forecast consulted. The transportation arrangements were of great interest. They were to ride in two vehicles, Captain Benwick's new sports car, a Silver Arrow, and Charles and Mary's family van which could accommodate more passengers plus the luggage. But because Mary insisted on sitting between Ann and Louisa in the van while Charles drove, Ben and Frederick found themselves destined to ride alone in the sports car.

"But only as far as after the Bridge," insisted Louisa. "I want to ride in the Silver Arrow the rest of the way!"

Ann knew that Louisa's statement was prompted not so much by the attraction of the little sports car as it was the prospect of riding with Frederick.

Adam was not about to let his Henrietta go off without him and was happy to be included in the invitation to travel with the group. Only the threat of stormy weather clouded their spirits as the final preparations were made.

The morning designated for departure dawned cloudy and windy with a dark sky in the east. Most weather changes came from the west, so the travelers did not worry, but the senior Musgroves, who were to have charge of the children while Mary and Charles were gone, feared a "nor'easter" and suggested that the trip be postponed till a more favorable day.

"How can you enjoy the beach or visit any lighthouses if it's cold and rainy?" Mrs. Musgrove asked.

Louisa was quick to reply. "It's a quick moving low front, Mama. The storm will have passed by the time we get to Ludington. If we don't go now, we'll never get another chance."

Youthful determination prevailed and the two cars pulled away shortly after sunrise.

Ann always loved crossing the Straits on the big bridge. Riding along the approach which slanted upward toward one of the twin suspension towers was like taking off into the sky. Looking down, she could see the waters of the Straits all wrinkled with white caps like ribs of chenille on a blanket of blue. A lone freighter was plowing furrows at an angle to the waves as it headed down toward Chicago.

Mary began to complain. "I don't like this. I feel nauseated. Charles, slow down."

"This is the speed limit. I need to keep up with traffic. We can't go any faster or slower. We're driving on this open grating. That's why you hear the rumbling."

"Why didn't they build it with a solid roadway?"

"The grating lets the wind blow through it instead of putting extra strain against the supports." He began his sink-or-swim approach to Mary's fears. "Look down at that freighter, I think by its short length it's a salty."

Adam countered with, "Close your eyes and think of the Twenty-third Psalm."

Henrietta objected. "Adam, don't be so pious. All that *shadow of death* stuff is unnecessary."

Ann added, "We're almost across. You'll

feel better when we stop to eat."

Louisa tried to focus the conversation on their goal.

"Ludington is going to be so much fun. There's a lighthouse on the pier right at the beach, one that we can walk out to. Frederick says there's a big one in the State park north of town too, but there's no road to that one, and we'll have to hike to it. We should have time because we're not taking the ferry boat till evening."

As they approached Mackinaw City at the south end of the bridge, Mary seemed to have survived with very little actual distress. But Louisa became upset when the Silver Arrow sped ahead of them out of sight.

"We were supposed to stop for breakfast here in Mackinaw! Why did they drive on? Charles, speed up and catch them!"

"No way. The plan was to stop here at that Bridge View restaurant. They're probably there right now waiting for us."

They circled the main streets and stopped at the restaurant, but there was no Silver Arrow in sight. Charles surmised that they had perhaps stopped for gas and would be along by the time breakfast was ordered.

"We'll eat here, anyway. I need some coffee, and Mary can enjoy the view without being nervous."

The amount of pancakes Mary consumed seemed to belie her previous nervous stomach, and with the exception of Louisa, everyone seemed in good spirits after the meal.

Old Mackinaw Point Lighthouse stood across the park at the edge of the water only a couple hundred yards from the van, but Louisa was more intent on catching the Silver Arrow than strolling around the lighthouse, so the journey was resumed with no delay.

Chapter XI

Ludington is a charming town on the west coast of Michigan's lower peninsula. Because of its fine harbor, it was a busy shipping port in the lumbering days of the last century, and is still popular for its fine beaches, parks, and fishing. It is also the port for the only car ferry still crossing Lake Michigan between Michigan and Wisconsin.

It was not seen at its best, however, on the June day when the Uppercross party arrived there. Rain had drenched the streets, and angry clouds were still scudding across a gray sky before a strong wind.

Charles drove along the main street which ended at the waterfront. As he stopped at the beach parking lot there, they saw Ben and Frederick in the Silver Arrow.

In answer to Louisa's petulant questions about why they had not waited at Mackinaw, Ben explained that they had waited at the restaurant, but when the van did not arrive, decided that the rest of the party had already gone on; so they had hurried toward Ludington. There had been a misunderstanding as to the name and location of the rendezvous restaurant. Even Mary was calmed when she learned that Ben and Frederick had arrived in Ludington early enough to make dinner reservations at a fine restaurant overlooking the Pere Marquette Harbor.

Louisa admired the lighthouse at the end of the pier. The North Breakwater Light was a white three-story tower at the end of the L-shaped pier which extended about half a mile into the lake. The tower itself had flat sides which tapered like a pyramid and a lower ledge shaped like the prow of a ship.

In spite of the wind they enjoyed walking along the beach. The Lake Michigan surf was washing the shore with magnificent rollers, and the bracing air and exercise were refreshing after the long drive. Louisa headed toward the pier.

"Let's walk out to the lighthouse!"

But Ben and Frederick discouraged the idea. They had already gone part way out, they said, and the waves were actually washing up onto the pier, making walking dangerous.

"The wind may go down this evening. We can come back after dinner and see if it's safe to reach the lighthouse. This is June, and it won't get dark till ten."

As they were returning to the parking lot, a man in a dark top coat, carrying a cane, was approaching the stairs toward the beach. He was tall, with a fine crop of curly hair, quite gray, which contrasted with his youthful countenance. He drew back to give way to the ascending group, and as they passed, he looked at Ann with a degree of earnest admiration. She realized she was being admired, and as Frederick noticed the stranger's gaze, he turned around to look at her also. The sharp wind had given extra color to her complexion and a sparkle to her eyes. Frederick may have been thinking, "She really is the most attractive one of our group."

Dinner was an enjoyable interlude. Their table gave a view of the marina, which looked like a forest of little masts rising from the water, swaying in the wind in spite of the sheltered anchorage.

There followed a discussion of whether the wind had subsided or not, but after dinner they headed for the pier again. A flock of gulls picking at some refuse on the shore flew up at their approach, and bravely battling the wind, wheeled over their heads in graceful arcs. Louisa, enchanted with the birds and energized by the wind, called out, "Ann, I'll race you to the pier," and began to run.

Ann took up the challenge, but their movements were slowed by the force of the wind as well as by the effects of having eaten a hearty meal. Mary and Henrietta turned back to seek the shelter of the van, but the men continued to follow.

At the entrance to the pier, a posted sign warned DANGER SURFACE UNEVEN AND SLIPPERY WHEN WET.

Louisa was undeterred. "Look, the waves aren't so high now. Let's go out to the lighthouse!"

Frederick called, "No, Louisa. Come back! It's still slippery."

But she could not be persuaded to return. Ann stopped at the warning sign and Frederick ran past her in pursuit of Louisa, who ran on laughing as if her daring venture were great sport.

Frederick called, "Watch out! There's a hole there. Stop!"

But it was too late. Her foot slipped into the crack of a concrete slab, and she tumbled down onto the rocks at the edge of the pier.

Frederick scrambled down to get her and dragged a very wet and white-faced Louisa back onto the walkway. By the time Adam and Charles reached them, it was evident that Louisa was seriously hurt. She was gasping from the cold of the water and holding her right arm with her left.

Ann came up just as Louisa slumped over in a faint. Everyone seemed stunned. Ann took off her own jacket to wrap around Louisa and said, "Quick, back to the van. Dry clothes."

Frederick lifted her carefully and carried her to shore.

Ben said, "Take her to Harville's. It's close by and she can change clothes there."

Louisa regained consciousness but was going into shock from the pain. Mary was becoming hysterical, Adam was saying a prayer, and Henrietta was frantically trying to find Louisa's suitcase in the back of the van.

Frederick carried Louisa to the Arrow while Ben went toward the phone pole, then changing his mind said, "We can phone from the Harville Inn. Let's go there first. Charles, follow us."

Harville Inn was a Victorian styled bed-and-breakfast on Ludington's main street. Ben and Frederick were acquainted with John Harville from their Ludington Coast Guard days and knew John's parents operated the popular hostelry.

Mrs. Harville, a short, plump lady, welcomed them warmly, sympathizing with their plight. But because Mary seemed in the most distress, Mrs. Harville focused attention on her first. Then she saw Louisa's pale face and swollen arm.

"Oh my, oh my! Sit right here. How did you ever do that? I'll get some ice. You'll be wanting to take her to the doctor. The phones are out of order. I think the lines went down in the wind. Oh dear dear. Would you look at that! It's turning blue. I do believe it may be broken. Does it hurt terrible, Honey?"

As soon as Louisa was helped into dry clothes, ice was applied to her arm. Because she complained that her head was aching also, Mrs. Harville gave her some hot tea and wrapped her feet in a blanket.

Explanations and hurried introductions came next, and as Louisa began to rally, Mary demanded that something more be done for Louisa immediately.

Ben suggested driving Louisa right away to the hospital in Traverse City. Ben and Frederick would take her in the Silver Arrow while the others waited in Ludington with Mrs. Harville. The plan included canceling the evening ferry boat reservation and taking rooms at Harville Inn for the night instead.

Louisa, Ben, and Frederick left shortly. Mrs. Harville served tea "with a wee bit o' something in it to calm the nerves, you know." Adam politely refused and then glared at Henrietta as she accepted a cup. Mrs. Harville bustled about with tiny steps moving like an automaton on little wheels. Her tongue, which was activated by the same mechanism, operated without stopping. The warmth of her hospitality compensated for the triviality of her conversation, and as the group relaxed, Ann enjoyed looking around the room with amusement at the profusion of bric-a-brac. Every available nook and surface was covered with figurines, photos, arrangements of artificial flowers, and teddy bears wearing lace dresses and bonnets. One tasteful bouquet of fresh white carnations on a hall table was the only elegant touch among the tawdry kitsch. Ann estimated that the number of knickknacks in Mrs. Harville's home would rival the number of mechanical gadgets in Henry Von Russet's den.

While they waited anxiously for the phone service to be restored and to hear news of Louisa, Henrietta mused, "Poor Louisa. She's finally getting her ride in the Silver Arrow. But not in very enjoyable circumstances."

Chapter XII

At sunset the wind subsided and Ann invited Henrietta to go for a walk along the beach, but Henrietta declined, preferring to wait with the others near the phone for news of Louisa.

As Ann left the Inn, she could hear the blast of sound from the ferry boat, signaling its departure from the pier, and as she reached the beach, she could see the huge ship silhouetted against a red sunset sky as it sailed past the lighthouse. She envied the passengers who would be able to see the other lighthouse farther down the coast and perhaps catch a glimpse of the ghost light.

The peacefulness of the cool evening, and the smoothness of the hard packed sand at the edge of the waves tempted her to run along the beach farther than she had at first intended, and when she turned back, full darkness was descending. There was no moon, but the sky began to glow with an eerie greenish tint. Beautiful curtains of light waved and glowed all along the northern horizon. The aurora borealis was giving a theatrical display.

She was reminded of the legend from Turtle Island. In the golden age of the Indians the Great Spirit, called Gitchie Manitou, forsook the sky and came to live on the beautiful Turtle Island as his home, blessing it with abundant fish and game for the people. But when the Europeans came and spoiled its beauty, Gitchie Manitou flew away to the far north where he now dwells in the flaming light of the aurora borealis.

The beauty of the sky brought a longing for someone to share it with, and she thought of Frederick and his attempt to stop Louisa's headstrong run out onto the pier. She wondered if now he might concede that being persuadable might not be such a bad thing after all.

Returning to the Inn, she planned to announce an invitation to come out and look at the northern lights, but everyone had already gone to their rooms, and the living room was dark except for the light from the television. She decided to switch on the sound in order to hear the weather forecast.

As she went toward the set, she heard a

noise in the corridor, and turning toward the doorway, saw the tall man they had seen at the beach. He paused, and giving a slight nod, with almost a bow in her direction, said "Good evening," then passed on down the corridor.

His voice was smooth and low, and his look and warm smile seemed to convey the recognition that they had met before. Her answering hello was probably cold and impersonal, as it should be, she thought, toward a stranger who just happened to be staying at the same guest house; but she was curious as to his identity, and a little sorry she hadn't been nearer the door in order to make a comment about the weather or the sky and perhaps begin a conversation. She went up to her room with the assurance from the weather man that tomorrow would be fair and with the anticipation that she would meet the stranger at breakfast. Only the uncertainty of Louisa's condition and the fate of their vacation trip clouded the night.

The next morning dawned fair and calm, and the first thing Ann heard was Charles in the hallway talking on the phone. When she went down to the breakfast room she learned that Louisa had perhaps suffered a slight concussion in her fall, had been kept overnight in the hospital for observation, but was to be released this morning. The X-rays showed that her arm had indeed been fractured, but the cast was in place, and she was ready to travel home.

Henrietta wanted to join Louisa and assumed they would all head back to Uppercross as soon as possible.

But Charles had other ideas. "We've come this far, and I'm not going to drive back the same way. Louisa will be all right. She's in good hands with Ben and Frederick, and there's nothing we can do for her now. I say we take the morning ferry to Wisconsin and continue the trip. We don't need to stop at any other towns, but Frederick wanted us to see that ship museum at Manitowoc. Louisa plans to call here in a few minutes and talk with you."

They sat down to breakfast in a kitchen decorated with a hundred chickens. The tablecloth and dishes were patterned with hens, the cannisters on the stove were roosters, and there were baby chicks on the wallpaper border around the ceiling. Mrs. Harville's clucking commentary added to the theme and at the same time satisfied Ann's curiosity about the tall stranger.

"You mean the tall handsome man with the gray curls? Oh my, yes. He left early this morning. Came over from Manitowoc on the *Badger*, two days ago. Said he was on his way to Turtle Island. And he's quite the gentleman. So thoughtful. He noticed that I like flowers (You've seen that I have several bouquets around the house.) and he brought me the bouquet of real flowers you saw in the hall. He must be quite rich. I don't get real flowers very often. He's from England. A graduate of Oxford I do believe he said. You probably noticed his accent? So charming. His name is Elliott."

"He might be our cousin!" Mary interrupted. "My Aunt Jewell said a William Eliot was on his way to visit. He was supposed to be bringing a friend. Was he alone? Did he spell his name with two l's or one?"

"He was by himself, I'm sure. I do believe he spells his name with double letters. But you are Musgroves, aren't you? Oh, I see. Musgrove is your married name. But isn't that interesting! You've never met him? Well, I'll look at the guest book again where he signed his name. Paid with a very large tip, he did."

Only the ringing of the hall phone interrupted her chatter, and as it proved to be the call from Louisa, everyone remained silent. But Mrs. Harville closed the kitchen door, not only giving Henrietta privacy, but enabling her to continue her own monologue.

Henrietta returned and tearfully conceded that Louisa's wishes were for them to continue without her. Ben and Frederick were taking her back to Uppercross, where they would all meet after the trip. Charles looked quite satisfied that he had been proven correct in his decision. Adam was given the opportunity to put his arm around Henrietta and comfort her with cheerful words about the anticipated boat ride. Mary was relieved that she would not have to cross the bridge again. And they were all pleased that the weather forecast promised a smooth Lake Michigan crossing.

The next few minutes were a wild scramble to gather their belongings, settle accounts with Mrs. Harville, and drive to the carferry dock.

Even after seeing it from a distance, Ann was surprised at the size of the ship. Seven stories high and half a football field in length, the *Badger* was impressive. Originally designed to haul railway cars across Lake

Michigan, the huge belly of the ship now carried hundreds of cars plus semi-trucks and tour busses.

Charles left his van at the end of the long line of cars and went into the ticket office to pay the fares. Badger workers were driving the cars into the rear of the ship. Ann wanted to look at the items displayed in the ticket office with the thought of buying a souvenir for Louisa, but Charles urged her to hurry.

"You can buy any of those things on board. Let's go! We don't want to miss the boat!"

They climbed the gangway stairs in the stern of the ship and stood at the rail to watch the last few cars, their van among them, being driven into the hold. The deep horn sounded, lines were cast off, and the huge steel jaw lowered slowly to secure the deck gateway.

The ship began to move out from the dock. The water churned white from the powerful thrust of the engines, and hundreds of gulls swarmed and swooped to dive for the little fish that were stirred up in the churning wake.

Not wanting to look down at the water from that height, Mary went inside, followed by Charles and Adam. But Henrietta stayed at the rail a few more minutes with Ann to watch the receding shore.

"I'll bet Louisa and Frederick will be engaged soon. Maybe she'll have a ring by the time we see them again."

"It could be," replied Ann, at the same time hoping her own doubts on that score were valid.

Some jet skiers crossed and re-crossed the wake of the ship in order to feel the thrill of the bounce and slap of the waves. The ship passed close to the brick condominiums where people sat on terraces watching and waving to people on deck.

The *Badger* continued past the Coast Guard Station with its red roofs, then the rocky pier ending with the flat-sided white tower of Ludington Light. A few boat watchers and fishermen stood waving from the lighthouse platform. As the gap between ship and shore widened, sandy cliffs appeared in the distance, with the smoke from the ship engines painting a gray brush stroke above them along the horizon.

They were headed toward the Wisconsin sunset and everyone except Ann seemed to reflect the joyful *bon voyage* spirit.

Chapter XIII

Henrietta seemed to think Louisa and Frederick were a confirmed pair, but Ann noticed that Henrietta wan't so sure about her own attachment to Adam because of his strict lifestyle. Disagreements were continually arising. When the entertainment director announced a Bingo session in the main lounge, Henrietta eagerly went in to play, but Adam frowned his disapproval and left for the upper deck. Mary was delighted to win a *Badger* mug.

"I'll give it to Louisa as a souvenir. Listen! They're announcing karaoke. Charles, I dare you to sing."

"Not by myself. I'll sing if Adam will join me." He was confident that Adam could never be persuaded to sing in front of an audience with a music machine which was usually found in taverns.

But in looking through the list of song titles, Ann found "When the Saints Go Marching In," and believing that Adam may approve of a song with a religious theme, persuaded Henrietta to go with her and find Adam to see if he would accompany Charles.

They found Adam in the stern lounge watching a historical shipping video. He agreed to try the song, and Charles was forced to make good on his promise. Charles first tried protesting, declaring he couldn't carry a tune at all, but when he finally rose from his seat, the audience encouraged him with loud clapping.

Adam's fine baritone voice was not strong enough to keep Charles on key or keep him from lagging behind the phrases as they appeared on the screen, but Charles' laughter and self deprecation throughout the number won everyone's applause. Even Adam was laughing by the time the music stopped. Charles and Adam were both awarded little sailor caps for their efforts, and the merriment helped bring everyone into accord. Henrietta's warm admiration of Adam showed in the look she gave him. She was proud that her "preacher boy" could join the crowd and have a good time.

Ann was secretly pleased that she herself had been the catalyst in bringing Adam and Henrietta together.

A uniformed man came up to their table inquiring if they were the Musgrove party. He was Captain Whalen, Frederick's friend. Frederick had informed him they would be aboard and may like to see the wheel house. They responded with happy agreement and the last half hour of the trip was spent there with eager questions on their part and of interesting information from Captain Whalen. He explained that the *Badger* was the last steamship on the lakes and reminded them to notice when they arrived at the dock the huge piles of coal used to fire the engines.

The four-hour crossing was ending. Henrietta asked about the harbor lighthouse and was told it was called the Manitowoc Breakwater Light. It was built in 1918 and has been automated since 1971. She took a photo for Louisa and noted down the name and place.

They had only a short wait while the van was driven off the carferry. Red-coated attendants pointed the way to downtown Manitowoc and the area attractions. The Maritime

Museum was absorbing and educational, and it sharpened their appetites for dinner, which was taken in a restaurant overlooking the harbor.

Their motel was clean and comfortable but lacking the hospitality of a bed and breakfast. Charles declared it a plus, not to have to listen to Mrs. Harville's chatter.

The next morning everyone was ready to return to the Upper Peninsula; consequently, the charms of Green Bay, Wisconsin, were passed over in favor of Escanaba, Michigan. When they arrived there, Mary declared they must be traveling in reverse because the main street is named Ludington Street, and the big hotel with medieval-looking cupolas where they ate lunch was House of Ludington. As their journey drew to an end, the only regrets were that Louisa was not with them and that they had been unable to see any ghost lights.

Late that evening they arrived in Uppercross and went directly to Huntingdon Lodge. They found Louisa ensconced in a big pillow-chair, with Ben hovering close by. As they entered the room, he put down a book of poetry and came to greet them. Most of the noise and excitement following was due to the welcome of Charles and Mary's little boys, and the update on Louisa's condition by the elder Musgroves.

And where was Frederick? He had been called to the Coast Guard Station at Tawas, but Ben was able to prolong his own leave and had been so attentive and helpful to poor Louisa.

"Ben has been educating me about the great poets," explained Louisa, "and I'm enjoying it so much."

Ann could see that it probably was the extra attention from Ben as well as from the whole household that was so gratifying to Louisa.

And so much for that advice she had given him about avoiding poetry in favor of prose! With someone to share it with, poetry could be very healing indeed, for a broken arm as well as for a broken heart.

At Uppercross Cottage a message from Aunt Jewell was waiting for Ann, urging her to come to the Island as soon as possible. Ann wanted to question the reason for her urgency, but wanting to avoid any disagreements, she packed and said her goodbyes. She had mixed emotions. It would be good to be on the Island again enjoying the solitude of the forest walks, and the sociability of the summer vacation atmosphere, but there was a kind of nostalgia for the associations of Uppercross and the renewed hopes the springtime there had brought.

Chapter XIV

In the long ago time when the earth was new, the Great Spirit Gitchie Manitou created all the fish, the birds, and the animals. The fish swam away in the waters, the birds flew away into the sky, and the animals went to find the place each liked best.

The turtles went very slowly. The biggest turtles went toward the salty seas. One huge turtle remained with the smaller ones and said he would lead them to the inland waters.

After many moons they came to Lake Erie, where the flat shores and shallow water made a fine home. The small turtles stayed there, but the big turtle wanted to go farther. He saw strange lights along the northern horizon which lured him to continue his journey.

None of the others wanted to go with him, so he journeyed on alone. He swam up the long Lake Huron. The autumn winds came and the water grew colder. At the narrow straits where Lake Huron joined Lake Michigan he could no longer move. The water turned to ice and trapped him there. He froze to death, but his shell remained and over the years grew into an island which the Indians named Michilimackinac which means Great Turtle.

Today Big Turtle Island, at the junction of the sweet inland seas, is one of the great vacation spots of the world as well as a historic shrine. Its history holds dramatic stories of the Island as an Indian fishing ground, a home of Jesuit missionaries, a rendezvous for the French fur-trading voyageurs, and a strategic fortress location during the War for Independence and the War of 1812.

First a national park, then a state park, the Island attracted wealthy vacationers in the 19th century. They built huge houses on its bluffs and called them summer cottages.

When the first automobiles came to the Island and frightened the horses and the inhabitants, the Island commission issued a prohibition against them, a ban which remains in effect today. Except for emer-

gency vehicles, no cars are allowed on the
Island, and all transportation is by horse or
bicycle only. The ban enhances the charm of
the island with its picturesque cliffs, forests
of pine and cedar, and the little ferryboats
scurrying back and forth in view of the big
bridge and helping it to link the two peninsulas of Michigan.

Ann's departure day came with perfect
weather. The sun glittered off the waves that
were not quite whitecaps, the rooster-tail
ferry was throwing up its big plume of water,
and several sail boats were headed toward the
big bridge. A "thousand-footer" freighter
moved slowly along the distant horizon. From
her ferry boat Ann saw the familiar turtle-shell
shape of the island, then as the boat came
closer, the huge Grand Hotel with its long
veranda, the boxy red and black Round Island
Lighthouse, and finally atop the hill above the
busy harbor, the white-walled Fort Mackinac.

Aunt Jewell had inherited from Aunt Nettie, along with the magnificent Bluff Cottage,
her maid Mrs. Tomkins, the groomsman
McDowdy, the black mare Cabaret, and a
gray cat named Julio.

It was McDowdy who met Ann at the dock with Cabaret pulling a small flat-bed wagon.

"Your aunt wanted me to bring the Victoria, but I said you'd have bags to haul, and on a fine day like this you don't need a hooded carriage."

"No. Besides, I like to ride up front with the driver. You made the right choice. How've you been? Cabaret looks clean and silky. You take good care of her."

"Oh, yes. She's fine, and I am too, but your Aunt Jewell is harder to please than Nettie Eliot was. She's a stickler for proper appearances. Wants me to cut my hair, so it's up off the collar, you know, and give up my chewing tobacco. I told her I don't smoke or drink, and a man has a right to have a few little bad habits for enjoyment."

"It is hard to adjust to a new employer," said Ann. "But your good qualities will soon convince her you're worth keeping." Privately Ann admitted that McDowdy's sparkling blue eyes and merry smile almost compensated for his tobacco-stained and uneven teeth.

Bluff Cottage was one of the elaborate houses built on the West Bluff of the island during the 19th century. At twenty rooms on three floors, it was a veritable mansion, but like the others along the Bluff which were originally summer homes only, it retained the designation of cottage. It displayed the irregularity typical of a Queen Anne structure with its jagged eaves, projecting gables, railed veranda, and two round towers with conical roofs. At the rear, the porte co-chere faced a servant house and carriage-house stables.

Mrs. Tomkins was waiting at the porte co-chere as they drove up, her frizzy hair rising up around a white cap, and her red face alight with a smile at seeing Ann.

In the parlor, Jewell was arranging white lilacs in a Waterford vase. "I'm glad you're finally here, Ann. That was a foolish trip you made with the Musgroves. Poor Louisa will be in a delicate state of health for a long time. How did you leave Mary and the boys?"

"Except for Louisa's accident, the trip really went well. Mary is fine. How is Elizabeth, and is Penny still here?"

"I'm hoping that with your arrival, Penny will see that she is no longer needed. She was a great help in the move and re-organizing Nettie's things. Except for your tower room, everything is cleared out now." She finished placing the last stem and gathered the clippings into a towel.

Ann sat on the Victorian settee and prepared to hear more news. "Did Cousin Eliot arrive?"

"Mr. Eliot is staying at the Grand Hotel. His friend did not come with him as we had expected. But William Eliot is a fine young man—all that I'd hoped as far as appearance and manners. Very well educated too. He seems quite taken with Elizabeth. He went walking with her and Penny last night, and I hope he will dine with us tomorrow. It will be quite nice to have an even six at table."

The top floor of the west tower of Bluff Cottage was Henry's domain. Here he had installed his computer with its accessories, his tinkering bench, and a half dozen or so of his more silent clocks from Woodleigh Hall. With his ponderous brass telescope mounted on a tripod near the curved window, he could watch the shipping of the Straits of Mackinac, and by consulting his reference books, identify the domestic and foreign vessels by their flags.

The top floor of the east tower was the storage area for Nettie's cartons of old papers. The receipts, statements, canceled checks, and old documents were stacked in a double tower of boxes pushed back near the window to make room for a narrow bed with crocheted ivory coverlet. This room had been saved for Ann, and she noted that she must accept a late-comer's fate of occupying the most cramped quarters. Elizabeth and Penny had a suite on the second floor with canopied beds and private bathrooms.

But her window did command a fine view over the houses along the sloping Bluff road toward the west end of the Grand Hotel. Beyond it was a glimpse of the harbor and in the distance a bit of Lake Huron. The gray cat Julio seemed to think the room belonged to him also, as he spent most of his day there perched on the topmost box, sleeping in the sunlight or watching the gulls which sailed past. He jumped down, and after stretching gracefully, brushed along Ann's leg in friendly greeting.

Chapter XV

Ann already knew that outside of one's own circle there is very little interest in another person's affairs, and although Uppercross and Big Turtle Island were only a few miles apart, they were entirely separate worlds. But she expected a little more curiosity and sympathy than she received at dinner that night. They sat at the oak table in the formal dining room enjoying the steak and mashed potatoes that Mrs. Tomkins had prepared.

Uncle Henry was the warmest in his greetings. "We're glad to have you back, Ann. You'll have to tell us all about your trip to Wisconsin."

"I went to Milwaukee once," put in Penny. "There are some grand houses there, but as for summer homes, I think Big Turtle Island cottages are bigger. And Bluff Cottage is probably the biggest, isn't it?"

"Except for the Governor's Mansion," said Jewell. "I hope to get a closer look at it next month if the Governor's wife invites us to tea. All the older islanders get an invitation, and I expect I'll receive one in Nettie's name. I hear that the First Lady has installed wall-sized mirrors in the parlor. I do hope she hasn't gone modern with the decor."

Elizabeth agreed with her. "I'm glad most of the cottages are keeping the Victorian interiors. Except for too much bric-a-brac, I think Aunt Nettie had good taste in that respect."

"I love the Tiffany lamps here," said Penny.

Here Ann tried to put in a description of the kitsch at the Ludington bed-and-breakfast inn, but she was cut off by Penny's next comments.

"You'll have to meet Mr. Eliot. He has excellent taste. He's from England, you know, and he declared the parlor here has just the right amount of fringe and tassels. Isn't that right, Elizabeth? 'Just the right amount of fringe and tassels,' he said. He's coming to dinner tomorrow."

Henry, having had enough Tiffany and tassels, excused himself from the table, and after dessert the women continued their conversation in the parlor.

Although Jewell accepted television as a necessary modern vulgarity, she kept the set in a rococo cabinet with doors that could be closed to conceal the screen. But toward the end of the evening, the Eliot women were gathered around the open cabinet to watch the evening news program when they heard a knock at the front door. Who could be calling so late?

Penny jumped up and opened the door to admit Mr. Eliot himself. "I'm sorry to call so late, but I was taking my evening stroll and happened to see your light. I decided to inquire if you were all right after last night's walk in the wind."

He was ushered into the room, and Ann drew back in surprise as she saw that he was the very same man they had seen at Ludington. He also seemed surprised, but not more astonished than pleased.

Jewell quickly turned off the television, closed the cabinet doors, and came to welcome the esteemed cousin and introduce him to Ann. He was very good looking and nattily dressed in a navy-blue blazer bearing an embroidered collegiate crest. His voice and manners were smooth and pleasant, and the conversation was definitely improved by his presence. She could think of only one other man whose personality could be so pleasing.

After he and Ann explained to the others where they had seen each other, he inquired her opinion of Ludington and of the carferry. The others were now suddenly interested in hearing more about the circle tour and Louisa's accident.

He regretted that he had not asked Ann's name at the inn. "I did not want to seem ungenteel or too forward," he explained.

Elizabeth in her cool elegance had little to contribute, and Ann watched to see if Mr. Eliot looked at her more than at the others, but his polished manners showed an equal attentiveness toward everyone.

The grandfather clock began to strike eleven, and everyone seemed surprised that the evening had passed so quickly. Mr. Eliot again apologised for calling so late, and in bidding them good night expressed his eagerness to see them again at dinner the following evening.

Ann had not supposed that her first evening on the Island could have passed so pleasantly.

As she was coming down the stairs to

breakfast the next morning, Ann felt that there must have been another polite pretense on Penny's part, offering to leave Bluff Cottage, because she heard Elizabeth say in a half-whisper, "Oh, no, she is nothing to me compared with you."

And as Penny noticed Ann, she asked, "Would you rather have the second floor rooms? I don't mind the stairs to the tower if you want to trade."

Ann declined graciously, really preferring the view from higher up, and Henry again insisted that Penny remain. " You want to be here for the Lilac Festival, and there's that big costume dance next month. What is that affair called, Jewell?"

"The French Masque. It's always held at the Grand Hotel ballroom. It's by invitation only." She had added the last statement rather coldly as she set down the coffee pot.

But Elizabeth quickly added, "You'll be included, of course. And at the end of the summer there's the Bridge Walk. We won't be moving back to Woodleigh Hall until after Labor Day."

The matter seemed settled, and Jewell finished her breakfast in silence while the others chattered on about the parade and the foot race to be held in conjunction with the Lilac Festival.

Regarding the foot race, Elizabeth and Penny decided they would walk the course, but Ann preferred the 10K run, which would be a six-mile circle along the main street with a climb past the fort to the top of the island. She asked Elizabeth and Penny if they wanted to join her in a training run after breakfast.

"Oh, no," Elizabeth replied. "We're just doing the walk. I don't like getting all sweaty going up that hill."

"And don't make me try that race-walking again, Liz," added Penny. "I can't wiggle my fanny and pump my arms like you're supposed to. What are you going to wear?"

The conversation declined into matters of wardrobe, and after finishing her peanut-butter toast, Ann excused herself to do a run around the Island.

Big Turtle Island is about eight miles in circumference, and the road following the shoreline is relatively flat. The island's status as a park had kept the housing outside of town to a minimum, and except for a new resort hotel on the far side of the island, the circle route remained wooded with pleasant views of the shore. Ann decided to go around the Island in a leisurely jog for distance training, omitting any sprints or hills. The morning was fair with a brisk breeze off the water, and in spite of the cool air, she soon became thirsty and regretted that she had left her water bottle behind. Approaching New Shore resort, she noticed a service road to the rear of the hotel and followed it in hopes of finding a water hose or a delivery door where she could beg a drink.

In an alcove behind the building three dining-room employees were taking a cigarette break. One man opened the back door and directed her toward a kitchen where she could hear the noises of dish-washing machinery and the clatter of lunch preparation. As she came back out and tendered her thanks, a woman called out, "Ann Eliot! Is it you? Where have you been?"

She was Marie Smith, a friend from Ann's Grand Hotel waitress days. They were delighted to see each other again, and began to exchange a quick review of their activities and whereabouts in the five years since they had met. Marie had grown plump and pale since their summer together, and although they both laughed at their similarity of short hair cuts, Ann privately observed that Marie must have had a less fortunate life during the last few years.

"I'm Marie Evans now. I never did finish college. I've been living with my mother in Detroit. I'm lucky to get this summer job on the Island, and I plan to go back to State U. in the fall. What about you and Frederick? Where is he?"

Just as Ann began to explain, the kitchen boss appeared at the door with a reminder that morning break was over and help was needed inside. Ann promised to time her next training run for Marie's break time on another day, and they parted with a farewell promise for a longer get-together.

Chapter XVI

The dinner that night was a success in everyone's opinion except Jewell's. She kept her opinion to herself, but was becoming quite impatient at the slow progress of her plan to rouse interest between William Eliot and Elizabeth. She had seated him directly across from Elizabeth, giving him a full view of her blonde charm. And Elizabeth was radiant in soft blue and crisp white, but it was Penny Clay who seemed to monopolize most of his attention. Her smiles and coy manner, her questions about his Christ Church College at Oxford, and her readiness to laugh at his *bon mots*, definitely drew his focus. Ann thought that Penny was fluttering her long eyelashes a little too much, but secretly admired her skill at flirtation.

Jewell's frowns grew more severe as the roast beef diminished, but her expression softened as Mr. Eliot began to direct his questions toward her.

"Mrs. Von Russett, when does the season end here, or do people remain on the island all winter?"

"The official end of the season is the end of October when the Grand Hotel closes, but a few people with permanent homes stay here all winter. Of course, the most important people have homes down-state. Even if Bluff Cottage were winterized, I'd never stay here; the noise of the snowmobiles would be terrible."

"Do the ferries stop running in the winter?" He leaned toward Jewell with genuine interest in the topic.

"One line manages to operate until January, but the island is quite isolated until the ice bridge forms. That may not happen until February. My sister used to fly to the peninsula to do her shopping."

"I'd be afraid to go on the ice," announced Penny. "I've heard that snowmobiles have broken through and gone down."

"If they stay between the lines of Christmas trees put out to mark the ice-road, they're safe," explained Elizabeth.

"And are there no horse-drawn sleighs?

Don't the horses remain on the island for the winter?"

Henry seemed to be the authority on that topic. "Most of the horses are ferried back to farms in the U.P. for the winter, but several hundred are kept here to pull the wagons."

From the topic of wagons the conversation settled on the carriages and then on the little Victoria that Jewell had inherited. She planned to ride to church in it the next day and regretted that it held only three people comfortably. Henry never attended church, and Jewell was hoping that Ann and Penny would choose to walk so that Mr. Eliot and Elizabeth could ride with her in the Victoria.

But Mr. Eliot said he would rather walk and deferred the pleasure of riding in the Victoria till another time so that Elizabeth and Ann could ride.

Ann quickly spoke her preference for walking also, adding that she needed the exercise as part of her training regimen. The matter was resolved, to Ann's delight and Jewell's discomfiture, with the plan for Elizabeth and Penny to ride in the carriage while Mr. Eliot accompanied Ann on foot.

That night Ann was wakened by the sound

of rain on her tower roof. The hard down-pour gradually lessened to a softer drizzle, but she could not go back to sleep easily. In a restless half-slumber she dreamed first of Frederick, then of Elizabeth and Penny, and finally of Nettie.

Frederick was wearing a dark peacoat and standing on the deck of a Coast Guard Cutter. (She realized later that people do dream in color because she remembered the wide red stripe down the prow of the ship.) He was looking out to sea as if searching for something. She had the impression that the water was deep and very cold.

Elizabeth and Penny were wearing ankle-length slickers and walking through the rain, holding hands and laughing. The sensation was that their laughter seemed rather secretive as if they were sharing a private joke.

The most vivid dream was of Aunt Nettie. She seemed to be climbing a stairway which ended at a locked door. When she tried to turn the doorknob, the door would not open; so she turned around and descended the stairs.

By remembering their daily activities, dreamers can usually find the elements of their night visions. Ann realized that the cold water around Frederick's ship had been generated by the extra chill in her room from the rainy night. And the sound of the rain had produced the Elizabeth and Penny sequence. But what had created the Aunt Nettie episode?

As she got out of bed, the stack of boxes not only indicated the origin of the Aunt Nettie dream, but they also triggered another thought: the missing letter. What if Frederick had written to her and the letter had come here after Ann had left for college and Aunt Nettie had concealed that fact? Her first reaction was a denial; Aunt Nettie, although strict and autocratic, was never deceitful. She and Jewell had guaranteed that Frederick was a playboy who never had serious intentions and that he would never write. But if he had, they would have granted him the benefit of a better opinion. And they had never indulged in the I-told-you-so stance of their justified assessment. Ann did remember only one later reference Jewell had made regarding "that giddy gang of college kids" with the comment, "You're well rid of that carriage-driver boy."

But the mystery of Frederick's comment at

the Huntingdon party still haunted her. The remote possibility of a letter from him remaining in Aunt Nettie's stack of old correspondence drove her to begin searching the boxes. She soon discovered that Aunt Nettie had been very methodical in her filing; each box had a different color label and each year's papers were arranged in a different box, but the pertinent focus of her search, the boxes from five years previous, contained at first glance, only business papers, and she would have to examine each envelope for any personal correspondence that could be hidden among them.

She placed one box on the bed and began to dig into it. Julio jumped up and into the box as if to help. She put him onto the floor where he paced with his tail twitching as if annoyed. But before continuing, she realized that she would have to defer the search to a later time because William Eliot would soon be arriving to escort her to church.

She felt rather foolish afterwards at breakfast because Jewell explained that she had already gone through all of Nettie's boxes. There was no personal correspondence that had been saved. Looking severely at Ann she added, "There was nothing pertaining to you." The old rule, she said was to save business papers for only five years. "We've already examined and dumped the oldest boxes, and to make more room for you in your room we can throw out the next layer. I believe the green-label boxes are from five years ago. I'll have Dowdy bring them down next week when the trash wagon goes by."

Mr. Eliot arrived early with his black umbrella, and because of the rain, was subjected to Jewell's suggestions before he and Ann could leave.

"Why don't you have the Grand Hotel take you in the coach? Or, because it's still early, Dowdy can drive you in the Victoria and then come back to get us."

But he and Ann repeated their intention to walk, displayed their thick boots and rain gear, and started off.

Chapter XVII

William Eliot was very agreeable and attentive to Ann during the walk, and their conversation was filled with polite trivialities. He expressed his pleasure at having her to himself and hinted that he would like to have her company on a more permanent basis.

"And you must call me Will. We are cousins, after all, and now we are close friends. No more formality."

Ann asked herself why his attentions made her uneasy. There was nothing she could criticize in his appearance or manners, and there was no reason to question his character. But he was almost too smooth, too agreeable. He had no strong opinions for or against anyone or anything. He expressed no distinct preferences that made him unique. She attempted to find a subject on which they could disagree and tried to test him by tricking him into expressing a view-point.

"The summer tourists are so obnoxious, don't you think? The streets are becoming so crowded, and they almost run over people with their bicycles."

To which he replied, "I suppose we must tolerate them for the sake of the economy of the island."

She tried again. "Do you like the smell of the fudge-making all along this street?" (Ann personally loved it and the rich candy which produced the heavy aroma.)

"I imagine it lures the tourists to buy extra to take home."

Ann ceased her questions and wondered if her doubts about William Eliot were only a result of her preference for another man, one who seemed more open, more candid. Why did she imagine that William Eliot's smoothness was only a facade?

The church was still quite empty when they arrived, and Ann led the way to the family's accustomed pew near the front. The church began to fill, and after the altar candles had been lighted, a stir was aroused by the entrance of somebody special. Heads turned and muted whispers could be heard. Someone of importance must be coming down the aisle.

It was the grand lady Jewell Von Russet herself and her beautiful niece Elizabeth Eliot. Jewell wore a huge pink hat trimmed with lace and flowers which matched her pink dress and shoes. Her classic features and tall dignity endorsed the suitability of the hat, which would have looked comical on anyone else. Elizabeth was resplendent in a pure white linen suit. She wore no hat, but her long blonde hair with slight curl at the ends complemented her fair features and the effect was quite as stunning as her aunt's more splashy ensemble. Little Penny, plump and freckled, followed behind in a brown and white polka dot dress.

William and Ann moved toward the side of the pew to make room for them, and the opening hymn began. Jewell's awareness of the attention she had received was only a brief pleasure because she soon became disturbed by the way the service was being conducted. The celebrant, the priest, and the reader were all women, and moreover the text being used was not the King James Version of the Bible.

Her irritation was quite evident. She had been one of the last to accept the newer version of the Prayer Book, and always preferred the classic wording of the scriptures. Why must it now be "Faith, Hope and Love" when for four hundred years it has been "Faith, Hope and Charity?" She determined to speak to the vestry again about the importance of preserving the proper traditions.

Ann, on the other hand, enjoyed the scripture readings. The high sweet voice of the reader saying, "Love bears all things, believes all things, endures all things" found an echo in her own heart.

At the point in the service where greetings are exchanged among the congregation, Ann turned to greet those in the pew behind her and had a sudden jolt. She caught a glimpse of a tall, wavy-haired man toward the back of the church. Frederick? But she was unable to confirm that recognition for sure. She moved back and forth trying to see through the crowd in the intervening rows, but was unable to get a better look.

During the rest of the hour she was unable to concentrate on the service at all as she planned her escape via the side aisle to make a fast exit to the rear of the church.

It was indeed Frederick, waiting just outside on the steps and holding a huge green and white football umbrella. Because he had been watching her since he arrived, he had the advantage of Ann with time to compose his greeting. But both displayed a lack of composure as they met.

Ann blurted out, "Frederick! I thought your church was St. Anne's!" Then she upbraided herself. *How boorish of me! That isn't the way to welcome him to Trinity Church.*

"I hoped you would be here. I thought I might see you here." He spoke hesitantly and appeared quite ill at ease.

"When did you come? How long are you here for?" *My face must be red. That isn't the right thing to say.*

"I return to Charlevoix this afternoon. But I'll be back next week for the race. Do you plan to run?"

"Yes." And here they were interrupted by the arrival of William Eliot. "Frederick, this is my cousin William."

Frederick remembered the distinguished-looking man from the Ludington beach, and after they shook hands, Frederick inquired about the rest of the family.

William took Ann's arm possessively. "Mrs. Von Russet is here, but she's taking time to talk over some church matters in the parish hall. You can join them there for coffee."

"I was hoping to walk home with Ann. I brought my super-size umbrella." He suddenly felt out-classed and a trifle ridiculous.

"I'm taking Ann home in the carriage. Her Aunt Jewell told us to go on because she will be a while longer. Oh, here's Dowdy now. We won't make him wait. Come, Ann." And William put his arm around her shoulder and led her masterfully down the stairs to help her into the carriage.

She wanted to object but could express no reason for doing so. She would rather talk longer with Frederick, but William commanded, "Home, Dowdy!" and the carriage began to move away.

"Will I see you next week?" she called back to him.

He only waved, and her last glimpse was of a forlorn Frederick standing alone in the rain under his huge umbrella.

Chapter XVIII

At Bluff Cottage she had to wait patiently and make polite conversation with William while Dowdy made his second trip to bring the others home. When they arrived, Jewell insisted that William stay for tea. "You did not have a chance to try the little cookies that Mrs. Sappenfield always bakes for Sundays. But we have some of Mrs. Tomkin's tea cakes here. You must have some."

Ann excused herself, pleading a headache, but instead of going to her own room, went to the west tower where she knew she would find her Uncle Henry. He was seated near his telecope by the window, studying his Great Lakes Shipping book. "Too much rain. I can't tell if that salty out there is the Liberian ship they said was coming through today. Could've identified it if I'd looked sooner, but I was busy on the computer and it got by me."

"Have you been talking with Charles on e-mail? I want to know how Louisa is. Have Ben and Frederick been staying at Huntingdon?

"Ah ha! Wondering about your boyfriend Ben? I assumed he'd been writing to you. Charles says that he talks about you and is reading some books that you recommended." Henry winked and chuckled as if being in on a great secret.

"But is he still there at Huntingdon?" Ann did not explain that it was the other young man she was really interested in.

"I think both Ben and Frederick are stationed at Charlevoix, but they drive to Uppercross and Huntingdon on their days off. Here, have a seat. You can e-mail Mary right now."

"No. I won't interupt your work. Mary never uses e-mail, anyway."

Henry seemed surprised. "She writes to Jewell, I'm sure."

"Oh, she phones quite often, but she talks mostly to Elizabeth. I'm more interested in how Louisa is recovering."

"Charles does all the business arrangements for his folks, so I'm pretty sure he's in close touch with the Lodge and would've said something if Louisa wasn't doing fine. Come look at this ship through my scope. It's clearing up toward the east and here comes a thousand-footer. Let's check the book to see which one she is."

"Are the Coast Guard ships in your book?"

"Sure. Here's a picture of the big ice breaker. She's a pretty important one."

Ann spent the next half hour looking through the telescope and the book, then thanked Henry and went to her room.

That night she dreamed again of Aunt Nettie. It was the same dream of the locked door and the descent of the stairway. Ann had the feeling that Nettie's demeanor was one of sadness and regret rather than frustration or anger at the locked door.

During the next few days it became evident to Jewell that William Eliot was more attracted to Ann than to Elizabeth. She was mystified that the glamorous Elizabeth exhibited no inclination for her handsome cousin either. At first Jewell was worried about Penny Clay with her winsome wiles, flirtatious talk and come-hither glances, but all those machinations seemed lost on

William, who more and more turned his attention toward Ann. Jewell admitted that Ann had really improved in appearance since coming home from college. Getting away from the books and taking more exercise in the fresh air was doing her good, and if it was to be William and Ann instead of William and Elizabeth, she would do what she could to encourage the match. She dreamed of an Eliot wedding with Eliot grandchildren to follow. The great name of Eliot would be carried on.

Ann became more and more uneasy with the knowledge of William's attention. He was a frequent visitor, and she remained courteous to him in the presence of others, but she sought excuses to be gone when he came to call.

Visits to Marie at the New Shore resort made an excellent getaway. Ann enjoyed seeing her old friend, and the visits gave her morning runs a pleasurable goal. She cut up across the island to shorten the distance and enjoyed running along the wooded trails through the forest.

The two friends brought each other up to date on their lives since their Grand Hotel days, and in the brief minutes allowed on

Marie's work break, began to exchange more intimate confidences. Marie's life had been one of quite drastic ups and downs. She had married and moved to New York City. Her husband, a bright young accountant, rose rapidly in the world of finance and the couple enjoyed all the pleasures that wealth and society could offer. But he had died suddenly, and through lack of foresight on his part and due to the schemes of an unscrupulous friend, Marie had been left with a child and very little means of support. Her mother was caring for the baby during the summer while Marie worked on the Island.

Ann's difficulties seemed minuscule by comparison. She told Marie she was wondering how to discourage the attentions of her gallant cousin who was assuming he would be her escort for the French Masque.

Marie was thrilled to hear about the masquerade. "I'd love to go to the ball. I wouldn't need an escort. I love costumes and dancing. It's been so long since I've been to a really grand affair like that."

Ann wanted to grant her friend's wish. "I'll see if I can get you an invitation. My Aunt Jewell is pretty important in Island society and I'll ask her. It would be fun to plan our costumes together."

That afternoon Ann discovered, too late, that it was not the most propitious time to ask Jewell for a favor. Jewell was in a bleak mood brought on by two disappointments. First, the coveted invitation to tea at the Governor's mansion had not come, even though her neighbor Mrs. Sappenfield had received hers yesterday. And secondly, Penny Clay had been voted Queen for the Lilac Festival float of the Social Club.

"I cannot understand why Penny Clay, of all people, should be the one to ride the float in the parade! Don't they have eyes? Mark my words, Penny Clay did some conniving to get those votes."

Ann tried to soften her outburst. "Elizabeth does look more like a queen, but don't you think it's because Penny is more social? After all, it is the Social Club. Elizabeth always has been more quiet."

"Penny Clay is a nobody. Her clothes are a fright, and her grammar is atrocious."

"But she has a warm heart. People really like her. She and Elizabeth have been friends for a long time."

"I can't see why Elizabeth took up with

someone of such low class. And this Marie you're talking about sounds just like her. Unwed mothers are an immoral burden on society. We taxpayers are supporting her kind of people."

"She's a *widowed* mother, not an unwed mother. Her own mother is taking care of the baby while she works. She'll never go on welfare."

"Well, she's trying to get in where she doesn't belong. I have invitations for the immediate family, but not for every outsider who comes along."

Ann gave up. "I'll tell her the invitations are gone. I hope she'll understand." But Ann had another idea, a plan she would work on later.

Chapter XIX

That night sleep would not come. It was the night before the Lilac Festival race, and Ann wondered if she had trained enough, wondered if she would see Frederick, wondered if Louisa still had a hold on his affections, wondered if she could effect her plan to bring Marie to the ball, wondered if her recurring dream was a product of her own worries, or a message from Aunt Nettie in the spirit world. The last idea convinced her that her imagination was going too far. She finally turned on the light and read a few chapters in the mystery she had started until sleep took over.

She was wakened by Julio walking across her forehead, bringing the sudden realization that she had overslept. A glance at the clock showed that unless she began running now, she would not be at the start line before the gun went off. Why hadn't Elizabeth and Penny wakened her? They probably thought she had left long before; Ann was usually up and out to run before the others awoke.

She berated herself for her tardiness as she ran down the hill toward the schoolhouse where a crowd of runners was already assembled at the starting line. Stopping at the registration table to pick up her number and pin it on took only a minute, but she had no time to look for Frederick in the crowd or find her proper position in the middle of the pack. The starting gun went off, and she was forced to jog slowly through the walkers at the rear until the pack opened up, letting her advance at a faster pace. Penny and Elizabeth called a greeting as she passed them at the head of the walking contingent, and it was only after she passed some of the slower runners that she felt she was actually in the race.

Running from home to the start line had been a good warmup, but even at her best pace, she knew she would not see Frederick because he would be out in front by now, running with the faster men. Tourists stood along the main street cheering the runners.

Their festive spirit, along with the sunshine of a perfect day, finally energized her body and transformed her anxiety into the total enjoyment of running.

When the course turned left to climb the steep hill toward the East Bluff cottages, the pack thinned out considerably and advancing toward the front seemed less necessary. What's the use of killing myself on this hill, she thought, when I'm too late to place at the finish line anyway. The thought of not appearing like a laggard in Frederick's eyes was the main spur that kept her going.

Then she saw a woman in front of her wearing florescent pink socks and decided to use her old self-motivating trick: Just pass the one person ahead of you instead of thinking about the finish line. After you pass that person, pick the next one ahead as your goal and do the same.

She began to advance on Pink Sox and at the crest of the hill finally managed to get by her. Then Pink Sox took up the challenge and passed Ann. For a short while they ran abreast and exchanged comments. "Great day for the race," and "Love your socks."

Then Pink Sox pulled ahead with longer strides. Ann valiantly tried to muster more energy to do the same, but in spite of her own spurt of effort, had to admit that Pink Sox was gradually increasing the distance between them.

Toward the last third of the course she looked up to see some of the early finishers who were coming back along the course in a cool-down run. The third one was Frederick! His appearance quickened her breathing even more and she felt a surge of adrenaline, endorphins, and all the power that can emanate from the smile of an expected hero. He turned to run beside her, and encourage her effort. Their conversation was a series of short gasps with intervals of leg work between.

"Hi, Ann. You're doing great."

"I got a late start."

"You're almost there."

"This is deja vu, except I'm still running."

"No horse on the course this time."

"I think I'll make it."

"See you at the awards. I know you'll have one." And he turned away to run down a side path in order to avoid crossing the finish line again and fouling the timer.

She tried to rally a sprint for the last few yards, and she no longer cared about losing to Pink Sox. She ran into her chute, glad for the cheering and for the end of the hard work. The first person she saw after handing her race-number stub to the volunteer was Pink Sox. They shook hands. "Congratulations. I couldn't catch you again, but you made me try."

"Thanks. Knowing you were there gave me extra incentive."

The next person she spotted was William Eliot. He came through the crowd and gave her a warm embrace of congratulation.

"I admire your accomplishment. You have made me decide to take up running. You can be my teacher, but you must promise not to make me do six miles."

She made no answer as she concentrated on gulping water and eating an orange section from the finish-line refreshment table. She began looking around in the crowd for Frederick, but William took her arm and with an air of urgent secrecy, led her aside, saying, "Come with me. I have something to show you. It will take only a few minutes."

She began to object, but he led her up the path, behind the first row of buildings away from the school, and in her curiosity she followed. They turned the corner and she saw

Dowdy there leaning against the hitching rail in front of the tavern where Cabaret was tied with the Victoria carriage. He handed the lines to William, tipped his cap, and retreated into the pub.

William said, "Hop in. What I want to show you is just up the road a bit. "

"No. You can just tell me about it. I need to get back to the awards ceremony. I'm meeting some people there."

"The race master told me the awards would not begin for an hour. This will take only a few minutes. You need a rest after all that running." He took her arm and helped her into the carriage.

"I'm quite familiar with the island. I don't know what you can show me unless it's something very recent. I wish you'd let me go back for a jacket first. I'm really cooling off fast."

"How thoughtless of me. Here, take my jacket. I don't need it. It won't matter what you're wearing in the place I'm taking you."

The place was the Woodsy Restaurant, about a mile and a half into the forest. William must have made a reservation because a groom came out to lead the horse away, and a waiter came forward to inform him that his table was waiting.

"William, this is kind of you, but I've been here before, and I really cannot take the time to eat. I need to get back."

"Nonsense. We'll be back in plenty of time, and you can't tell me you aren't hungry after running six miles."

She had entertained the possibility of having breakfast with Frederick, but not wanting to spoil the great event her cousin was creating for her, succumbed to his entreaties. Their table was in a quiet corner alcove, out of view of the rest of the diners, and decorated with a special arrangement of roses and lilacs.

She planned to eat quickly and then would ask to leave immediately, but William began by ordering mimosas and telling the waiter they would study the menu for a few minutes first.

He drew from his pocket a small velvet box, the size of a ring box, and laid it on the table before her with a smile.

She rose in sudden alarm. "If that's what you're planning to show me, please don't. I really am not hungry. I thank you for the ride and the offer of breakfast, but I really have to leave."

"Wait!" His smile became a frown of disappointment, then of sudden anger as he reached out and grabbed her arm. She tried to wrest free of his grasp, but he gripped harder, even twisting her arm to force her back into her chair.

"Stop!" her yell was loud enough to bring a waiter hurrying to investigate, and as William released her, she jumped up and ran for the door, bumping into a second waiter who was carrying a tray and causing the mimosas to crash onto the floor. She threw off the jacket as she ran down the steps and turning into the forest, chose a path that would prevent being followed by a carriage.

She emerged later on the shore road, taking the long way back to the school toward the race finish line. Two bicyclists on the road paused and wondered at the woman who was running with tears coursing down her face as if she were being pursued by demons.

William had deceived her. The awards program had started soon after they had left in the carriage, and the ceremony had ended. The lot was nearly empty. A few volunteers were taking down the big overhead FINISH sign. Nearby an older woman was folding up a big pile of lilac-colored shirts. "Do you want a last year's shirt for half price?"

"No. Thank you. Is the race director here? I had to leave early and need to check the awards. I may have one."

The T-shirt woman directed her to a room inside where volunteers were packing up the rest of the paraphernalia. The race director said, "Ann Eliot? I think you got a third place for your age group. Your sister took your award home for you."

"How did Frederick Wentworth do?"

"First in his age group and third overall. He's quite a runner!"

Everyone had left. She wondered if anyone had seen her departure in the carriage with William. She wondered if Frederick would try to find her later.

The slowest and most difficult mile of Ann's day was the uphill walk back to Bluff Cottage alone.

Chapter XX

Over three centuries ago the Great Lakes area was in the hands of France. For five years a French soldier named Antoine de la Mothe Cadillac was commandant of the Fort at Michilimackinac.

He traveled to France to obtain a commission to build a fort at the Narrows (*Detroit*), the south end of Lake Huron where it becomes a river. He believed that a military position there would be a protection against the English and the Indians. On his return from France with the commission the Governor of New France entertained him with a fine banquet in his castle at Quebec.

As part of the evening's festivities the Governor brought a fortune teller to entertain the officers. She was a tall dark lady named Mere Minique, who wore a black hooded cloak and carried a black cat perched on her shoulder. She moved along the tables and collected a silver coin from each officer who wanted his fortune told. When she looked into a palm, the cat would lick her ear while she revealed amazing detail from the client's past. Amid the laughter of the soldiers was the uneasy feeling that the cat might be a familiar from the devil who was whispering the information to her.

When she came to Antoine, he said he did not want to hear about his past; he wanted to know the future. She took a silver vial from beneath her cloak and poured a heavy clear liquid from it into a crystal basin. When she held Antoine's hand, she looked into the basin and told him many strange things. She said he would journey far, would have many children, and would establish a great city.

But her predictions carried a dire warning. If he offended the Jesuit priests by selling brandy to the native peoples, there would be much bloodshed. "And if you become too ambitious, and offend the Red Dwarf (*Nain Rouge*), your children will not inherit your properties and you will die far away, hardly remembered in the city you establish."

Antoine did build Fort Ponchartrain and founded a city at the Narrows, where years later a big celebration applauded him , "Vive le Seigneur Cadillac du De Troit." But after that celebration as he was walking with his wife in the garden, an ugly dwarf with a red beard and red cloak approached them. Antoine's wife, remembering the prophecy, tried to draw him back, but Antoine struck the creature across the shoulders with his cane and said, "Get out of here, you Devil." The Red Dwarf gave a fiendish laugh and disappeared in a puff of smoke.

The city built by Antoine de la Mothe Cadillac was later taken by the English. He was arrested in Montreal and died in France. His city at the narrows burned to the ground, and when it was rebuilt retained only the name for the Narrows, Detroit.

Mrs. Tomkins met Ann at the door of Bluff Cottage with the news that a young man, Frederick Wentworth, had come to call on her. "No, he left no message. He did not stay. Mrs. Von Russett and Mr. Eliot are in the library waiting for you."

They were sitting tete a tete at the library table as Ann entered. Their complicity was obvious. Jewell had perhaps even suggested the breakfast ploy and loaned him the carriage. In her state of anger and exhaustion, Ann was unable to articulate her feelings, but her glaring look indicated her unsettled state and was a warning against any inquiry on their part.

Jewell tried to be cheerful, and after offering Ann some tea, turned the subject to the French Masque. "I was just suggesting that William go to the ball as Antoine Cadillac. I can get him the plumed hat and foldover boots. Won't he look grand?"

Ann glared at them, then said slowly, "No tea, thank you. And as for William, I think he would do better as *Nain Rouge*." She left the room without waiting for any comment.

A hot shower and some breakfast with Mrs. Tomkins in the kitchen restored Ann's composure but left her with a need to vent her feelings to a sympathetic ear. A visit to Marie was in order, and Ann walked to New Shore resort hoping to find her with some extra time off at lunch or willing to meet later in the afternoon.

Marie was eager to hear about the race, but wanted more time than she could take that afternoon. They arranged to meet on Monday, as it was Marie's day off and they could have lunch downtown at the Wharf-side Restaurant.

Even though all her thoughts were of Frederick, Ann dreamed that night of Aunt Nettie again. This time the dream was so vivid she seemed to hear steps on the stair-way. The locked door Nettie was trying to open was the one to Ann's room!

She wakened to see Julio sitting by the door, looking up at the doorknob as if wait-ing for someone to enter. Ann opened the door and turned on the light, revealing the empty staircase. Julio only wanted out for some midnight prowling around the big cot-tage. Noises can trigger weird visions, Ann thought. But she searched her own con-sciousness for any wisp of hidden memory that could be eliciting the recurring dream.

The Wharfside Restaurant was a cheerful, busy dining room in connection with the Wharfside Hotel. Ann and Marie asked for a deck table on the side where the ferryboat from Mackinaw City docked. The sunshine, the sailboats, and the gulls made a scenic backdrop hhfor their luncheon. It was fun to see the crowd of "Fudgies," as the tourists were called, getting off the boats with their children and their cameras, ready to explore Big Turtle Island. Unless they booked the carriage ride or rented bicycles, most of them got no farther than the main streets. But there were plenty of souvenir shops, clothing stores, historical buildings and an excellent bookstore to visit. The hardier among them walked up the long ramp to the fort and watched the entertainment there, complete with the firing of a cannon and a marching drill by uniformed soldiers.

When Ann related the unpleasant events of her race day, Marie commiserated with her, but expressed some sympathy also for the rejected suitor. "How disappointed he must be. He must have strong feelings for you, Ann. I would be flattered if a gentleman of his consequence showed that much interest in me."

"I was flattered," Ann replied, "until he almost broke my arm." And she showed Marie the large bruise on her left forearm.

"Yikes! Get rid of that man. He's no gentleman."

"I was almost comparing him with Frederick as to manners, but somehow I never did trust him. Why did I allow myself to be persuaded to go to the Woodsy with him! And to think I missed Frederick completely. He came to the cottage and they told him I was with William."

"Do you think Frederick is still seeing Louisa? You and Frederick seemed like the perfect pair five years ago. I can't believe he just forgot about you. He's a great guy. And such a sense of humor, too. Do you remember the dummy episode?"

"That must have happened after I left for school. Tell me."

"This big entertainer came to the Grand to do stand-up comedy. Collins, I think his name was. Anyway, he had all these jokes about the movie *Somewhere in Time* that was filmed here on the island. He was quite good with his monologue, but a real stuffed shirt, quite a pain to the hotel personnel. After his last show, Frederick, Eddie, Allan, and a couple others met him in the bar and flattered him until he thought he was the best comedian in the world. The boys would laugh uproariously at each joke, and ask him to tell another one. That went on until quite late. When he left to go to his room he was walking on air but holding himself up along the walls.

Eddie and Frederick had found a woman's wig in the lost-and-found and fixed up a dummy in Collins' bed. They even had an open suitcase on the floor with clothes hanging out.

The funniest scene was Collins at the main desk, telling them someone had gotten the wrong key and was in his room. But the real shocker, (He was as pale as a ghost, and you can believe sobering up fast), was that he told them 'She isn't breathing! I've called 911.' Well you can imagine what it was like when the Island police came and opened up the bed to see this wig and a roll of blankets. I suppose everyone is still laughing."

Ann was pleased to hear the story. She confirmed that Frederick always had a good outlook on life and believed no one should take himself too seriously. "Didn't you work with him in the office for awhile after I left?"

"Yes, and he was a card there too. One time when we were getting the payroll checks out, he wrote goofy things on the receipt half of some of the checks, of the guys he knew, of course."

Ann's eyes opened wide and she inhaled sharply. "Wrote on the receipt half of the checks? On the checks that were being mailed out? Marie, I just had a terrible thought! Today is trash day! I must get home! I'll explain later."

She threw down some bills to cover her lunch and dashed from the restaurant, leaving Marie in stunned amazement.

As she passed a table close by the door, a lady in a green straw hat leaned over and said to her husband, "Isn't that the same woman who dashed out of the Woodsy when we were eating breakfast there the other day? She must have terrible indigestion problems."

Chapter XXI

Pierre Massie enjoyed being the trash man on Big Turtle Island. Where else could a garbage man have such prestige? He loved his old horse Maud, who though aged, was patient and sturdy, and the quiet pace of his work, which was a contrast to the slam bang rush of motorized workers in peninsula cities. He was welcomed the way a postman would be elsewhere, because he was the only public servant to visit each house. The islanders all picked up their mail at the local post office, and though he made his trips just once a week, he was personally welcomed, and often delayed with offers of refreshment, in return for which he offered the latest information, information which we would classify as gossip, but his clients categorized as "news."

He knew about how the Von Russetts had inherited Nettie Eliot's Bluff Cottage and how their cleaning and re-organizing was finally diminishing the number of sacks they put out each week for disposal. But this week's trip had more than a modicum of interest.

He was on the way down the hill after passing the Bluff Cottage, when Miss Ann Eliot came running up the hill toward him in a panic.

"Pierre! Stop! Oh, I'm so glad I got here in time. I think there's a box that was put out by mistake. I need to have it. It's an old file box with a green label. Can you help me find it?"

Pierre was most gracious. "Sure. I remember loading such a box. Do you want me to drive it back up the hill for you?"

"Oh, no. Just set it down here. No, don't wait. I'll get it back to the house later." And she sat down beside the road and began frantically sorting through it, while Maud and Pierre continued on down the hill.

Mrs. Sappenfield, another cottager along the West Bluff, was puzzled to look out the window and see Ann Eliot sitting in the Sappenfield driveway digging through an enormous cardboard box and talking to herself while a gray cat circled slowly around her. "Checks, Checks, July, August, September.

Yes, September.

September, September. Yes, Yes, Yes! "

She held a small piece of paper in her hand, stared at it intently for several minutes, then pressed it to her heart. Standing up, she looked around as if in a daze, looked down at the box, replaced the lid, attempted to lift it, gave up, and walked up to Bluff Cottage as if in a dreamlike trance, leaving the box beside the road. As she walked, she read over and over,

"Dear Ann—Here is my letter. What a measly check. If you were on my payroll, I'd give you a thousand a week (Kisses, that is).

You are my only treasure. Let's plan to meet. I'm waiting for your letter. Better yet, call me at the Grand and give me your number.

Yours forever, F.W."

Here was the answer to the mystery. His "proof" that she had seen his note was the knowledge that the check had been cashed. But he did not know that Aunt Nettie had instructions to deposit any late-arriving check directly to Ann's bank account, rather than forwarding it to her in the mail.

Had Nettie deliberately withheld knowledge of the note? Or had she deemed a scrawled message on a check stub a mistake, part of an office memorandum, or intended for someone else? Ann would never know the real answer, but her stunned gratitude at finding the paper evolved into the question of what she should do next.

Her first impulse was to run to a telephone, call him and blurt out, "I found your letter! I'm sorry I did not call. Is it too late to start over?"

Then she realized that she did not know where he was or how to call him. The whole thing required an explanation. Would he believe that she had sent a postcard? Oh, why hadn't she sent a letter instead, with her proper return address? Oh, why had she ever let herself be persuaded that he would not try to contact her?

Reaching Capitalize cottage, she remembered that, first of all, Marie was due an explanation for her abrupt departure, and she tried to locate her by phoning the New Shore resort. There was no answer, but she left a message to call Ann at Bluff Cottage.

Next she tried to call Woodleigh Hall. Mrs. Croft would certainly know how to reach her brother Frederick. But Serle answered saying the Crofts were out, and could he take a message?

"No, I'll try calling again later today." Surely her sister Mary would be at home on a Monday, and the next call found her there.

After inquiring about Mary's health, she expressed concern for Louisa, hoping to gain information indirectly about Frederick.

"Well, I've had this sore throat," Mary began. "And you know my sore throats are always worse than anybody's. I hope to get over it by next week so we can all come to the Island for the ball. I have the blue-striped dress with the bustle that I wore for last year's pageant, which will do well if I add some fresh ribbons. I can't find the little matching parasol, but I've got time to look through the store room and locate it. You know how the men never like to dress up. Except for Frederick and Ben; they'll wear their Coast Guard uniforms and we approved that idea, but in order to get the others into the spirit, Frederick is directing us in a skit. Actually, it's Louisa and Frederick. Henrietta will tell the Marie-Therese story while Louisa, Charles and Adam act it out. Charles will be the Devil. It's hilarious. And of course that gets Charles into a devil costume and Adam will be the priest—good casting don't you think? Frederick will be here during his time off early next week for our final rehearsal. So we should be all ready for the French Masque. What are you wearing?"

"I guess I'll be a voyageur. I have the coonskin cap and leather leggings at Woodleigh Hall. I'm trying to reach the Crofts to have them send the things over, or bring them if they come. Tell Louisa I asked about her. I'll see you next week."

Ann remained in an unsettled state after the conversation. Louisa and Frederick, Louisa and Frederick was all she could think of. They were still together. How could knowledge of a message from Frederick to Ann five years ago have any effect on that?

Her despair deepened, but she was roused to action by the sound of the front door and Mrs. Tomkins admitting a visitor. Ann went down to the first landing of the stairway, and upon learning that the caller was William Eliot, declared herself "not at home" and escaped down the back stairway, out through the kitchen and down the hill toward town. On the way she stopped at the Sappenfield cottage and asked if Mr. Sappenfield could drag the box onto their porch to wait for the next garbage day. Then she ran down toward town and on to the New Shore resort.

Ann waited for Marie on the patio of New Shore Hotel. She sat at an umbrella table watching the waves, the gulls, and a few tourists who were walking along the shore looking for shells or interesting stones. One boy was trying to wade, but the rocky bottom of the shore kept him limping gingerly until he gave up the effort and sat down to put his shoes back on. The stony beach reminded Ann of the Petoskey stone and the fragment she had saved. She was lost in her reminiscing when Marie walked up laden with packages from an afternoon of shopping.

"Look, Ann, I have my costume for the French Masque ball. I'll be an Indian maiden. Just call me Hiawatha. Let me show you." And she proceeded to unwrap and display her finery.

Ann did not tell her that she had not obtained the necessary invitation. In fact, not telling her was part of Ann's plan. Ann conjectured that anyone appearing in costume would naturally be assumed to have an invitation. What "outsider" would go to the trouble to dress up in order to appear at a masquerade ball?

But Marie was more interested in hearing about the reasons for Ann's abrupt departure from lunch. After listening to the tale of the broken romance and the five-year-old note, she declared it an enchanting real-life love story, one that must have, really would have, a happy ending. She began to advise Ann on what to do to reclaim Frederick as her own. "First, forget the voyageur outfit. You must appear as a nineteenth-century belle with wasp waist and ample decolletage. Where can we get you a dress?"

But Ann explained that her appearance would not be the main obstacle. The difficulty was double: his attraction to Louisa and the interference of William Eliot. She related how William had also spirited her away from church in the carriage, while Frederick had stood on the steps with the big umbrella, intending to walk her home.

"Is your cousin so attractive that he can make Frederick jealous?"

Ann began to describe William's unique combination of gray curly hair and classic features, his British accent, his impeccable manners, his ability to charm old and young alike, and as she talked on, Marie began to breathe quickly, and add questions about him which confirmed that she herself had known him!

"Did he say he went to Oxford? Does he wear the tie or stick pin with the little cross and the blackbirds across the top?"

"He says that's for Christ Church College. The crest on his jacket is a red bull over wavy lines like water. That represents Oxford."

"Ann, unless this is a very unlikely coincidence, your cousin is Billy Oxbridge, the very man responsible for my ruination!"

And she continued to tell her how, after her husband's death, his best friend charmed her into a close relationship by using their mutual grief as a bond of friendship, eventually culminating in their engagement and marriage. Of no small concern was the fact that her baby girl would again have a father to love and to care for her.

But on the wedding evening he disappeared. There was a frantic search, a futile visit to the morgue to inspect the body of a car crash victim, and after the required time lapse, the filing with the police as a Missing Persons case. Nothing produced any clues until she received a call from her bank. Billy Oxbridge had cleaned out her bank account, including the amount from her first husband's insurance, and had disappeared completely. The car was found intact, parked at the Detroit airport, but no one of his name and description could be traced as to destination. That was two years ago. Her brother had hired a detective, and she had moved in with her mother, so the baby could be cared for while she went back to work. But there had been no trace of the missing bridegroom.

The afternoon was waning into evening by the time Marie had finished the entire tale of the Don Juan deception. The two women moved inside to the hotel dining room and continued their talk. Gone was the urgency of any Frederick-and-Ann plan; the immediate necessity was for Marie to see William Eliot and confirm his identity as the scoundrel Billy Oxbridge.

Chapter XXII

The Grand Hotel was built of Michigan white pine by two railroad companies in 1887 for wealthy vacationers who traveled to Big Turtle Island. It remains today as the showplace of the Great Lakes. Today's guests include families on vacation, honeymooners and convention goers, but the hotel maintains its Victorian charm and respectability, posting a dress code for dinner and charging an admission fee to enter the grounds for those not registered as guests.

Ann had convinced the uniformed attendant at the entrance that they had reservations for lunch, and she and Marie stationed themselves part way along the huge porch, but in view of the main door where William Eliot was expected to come out. Their plan was for Marie to be close enough to recognize him without giving away her own identity.

Both women were incognito with dark glasses and sun hats. Marie had covered her short brown hair with the black wig intended for her Hiawatha costume, and Ann had donned an uncharacteristic outfit of long skirt and high heels.

The famous porch, almost seven hundred feet long, was lined with flags, Chippendale style boxes of red geraniums, and furnished with rockers and lounge chairs giving a view of the gardens below, the Straits of Mackinac, and the big bridge in the distance. A few guests were strolling the length of the porch, while others were reading or relaxing as they enjoyed the view.

After an hour and a half, Ann decided on Plan B. She would wait inside near the elevators and stairway. As soon as she spied William, she would walk away down the long inside vestibule rooms to exit near Marie on the porch, passing by her. At that signal Marie would get up and walk toward the red-carpeted carriage landing. If the timing was right, Marie would come face to face with the suspected felon.

Ann chanced going to the main desk on the lower level first, to inquire if Mr. Eliot was in.

"No, don't ring, thank you. He knows I'll be waiting in the upper lobby for him."

She emerged from the stairway just in time to spot him leaving the elevator, headed toward the door. She would be too late! Trying not to run, she hurried along to her porch exit and passed Marie with a breathless warning, avoiding the impulse to look back.

But William was pausing in the doorway to put on a pair of gray gloves, probably conscious of the fine picture his well-tailored person was presenting to any onlookers. He stood at the top of the porch stairs long enough for the hotel carriage to pull up. The timing became perfect. Marie passed him and continued her stroll along the porch. "Close enough to touch him," she cried. "I feel like screaming! Yes, it is Billy Oxbridge in the flesh, the rotten, rotten man. Look at him in that gray suit! You can bet it was made by a London tailor and paid for with my Allan's money. Oh, Ann, I must call my brother. I can't stand it!"

Ann took her inside to mop the tears and remove the wig in the ladies' room. They strolled the hotel art gallery till Marie could control her emotions and go down to lunch where they schemed how they would expose and entrap the dapper felon.

Chapter XXIII

It was the breakfast hour at Bluff Cottage, and Mrs. Tomkins was bringing a fresh plate of scrambled eggs to the dining room when there was a knock at the door. Who could be calling so early? Ann thought first of William Eliot and wondered how she could make an escape, but she was relieved and pleased to know that it was the Musgroves. Mary and Charles were accompanied by Henrietta and Louisa, plus Trapper the dog, who came bounding in and headed for Henry as if to an old friend.

Jewell put on an air of decent welcome which became much warmer when she found that the Musgroves had not come with any intention of staying at Bluff Cottage.

"We came on the early boat," explained Mary, "and we'll be staying at New Shore. The Grand was already booked full. Our rooms at New Shore won't be ready till noon, so we decided to visit you."

Cordial greetings were being exchanged and additonal chairs were being brought to the table when a crash was heard from the kitchen, followed by a scream from Mrs. Tomkins.

Trapper, in an innocent but lively investigation of the kitchen had become caught in the dangling cord of the coffee urn and had pulled it to the floor, spilling coffee the length of the kitchen.

Charles and Henry dashed in to rescue the dog, calm Mrs. Tomkins, and help mop the floor. Trapper was relegated to the porte co-chere and tied there until the visit was ended. Jewell maintained her composure and assured her guests that nothing was broken, but the incident brought a decided chill to the breakfast and probably shortened the visit considerably. Louisa carried on cheerfully with as much information as she could impart between pieces of toast and jelly.

"Ben will be coming over in time for the party. I don't think Frederick or the Crofts are coming. Frederick said he has rehearsed us enough, and he will not be needed. You see my arm is doing fine, and I'll wear long sleeves for the party anyway, so the arm brace will hardly show. Our skit will be hilarious. You will love it. I will be Marie Therese and I've practiced my part so much I'm sure I can do it perfectly. You should see Adam with his grand gestures. Frederick told him to exaggerate and he really hams it up. You will laugh and laugh. And at the end there's a surprise. It will be so much fun."

After the visitors left, Jewell expressed her disgust at the boorish idea of bringing a dog into Bluff Cottage.

"Dogs are for children," she said. "I don't know why adults have to bother with them. And I don't know why Charles and Mary had to bring that beast along with them."

"It was either the children or the dog, according to Mrs. Miggs," replied Henry. "She wouldn't baby sit both. The children insist on having the dog inside, and Miggs put down her ultimatum."

"Well, I hope New Shore is prepared for damage if they admit dogs like that on the premises."

Ann felt a keen disappointment on hearing that Frederick would not be coming. "Weren't the Crofts invited to the Masque also? They seem like the kind of sociable people who would enjoy a party like this."

"I e-mailed them the particulars and told them they were on the list," replied Henry. "I'll check again to reinforce the invitation."

Soon after breakfast Ann climbed up to Henry's tower and found him engaged in an e-mail conversation with Admiral Croft at Woodleigh Hall. The latest message was that both Admiral and Mrs. Croft were looking forward to the French Masque ball and planning to come in costume.

What about Frederick? Admiral Croft said he did not plan to come. Ann, standing beside Henry as he sat at the computer, said, "Tell him to tell Frederick that someone he knows from five years ago will be at the party and wants to talk with him."

Henry had a better idea. "You tell him yourself. I'm not fast enough to type from dictation. Sit here and carry on." So she did.

Bluff Cottage: Admiral, this is Ann. Ask Frederick why he doesn't want to come to the party.

Woodleigh Hall: When we were talking

about the party at breakfast, he seemed out of sorts, and I think it's due to girl-friend problems. He said that the prettier a woman is the more fickle she turns out to be.

Bluff Cottage: Men are no better, especially sailors.

"One foot in sea and one on shore,
To one thing constant never."

Woodleigh Hall: Is that out of Shakespeare? I don't buy that one. Sophie and I have been married many years, and even tho' I've had one foot in the Lakes most of the time, I've been very constant.

Bluff Cottage: Yes, but Shakespeare also said that REAL love does not die. It does not even "bend with the remover to remove."

Woodleigh Hall: What does that mean?

Bluff Cottage: It means that true love does not end just because one person stops loving.

Woodleigh Hall: This philosophy is getting to be too much. You will have to explain that to Frederick yourself.

Bluff Cottage: Just tell him that someone he knew five years ago on Big Turtle Island is here again and will be at the party and would like to talk with him.

Woodleigh Hall: I guess I can remember to convey that message. But no more about fickle sailors or true lovers. You'll have to explain all that in person.

Bluff Cottage: O.K. That's all. I'm handing this back to Uncle Henry. See you at the party. This is Ann, signing off.

So Ann had to remain in hopeful suspense until the following night. She had not breathed a word of the sordid past of William Eliot because she and Marie were hoping to expose his treachery at the end of the ball.

But another cause for suspense arose that afternoon. Ann went into the library to determine the cause of the laughter originating there. She found Elizabeth and Penny rehearsing William Eliot in his role as Antoine de la Mothe Cadillac. He was wearing the big plumed hat, a black silver-buttoned coat, and the big boots with foldover tops. Elizabeth was advising him in his swagger-walk and telling him how to hold his cane.

Ann admitted to herself that he did cut a dashing figure, but now knowing his true identity, she saw the handsome cavalier as the essence of evil. It was also apparent that having despaired of securing Ann for himself, he was aiming for Elizabeth. His compliments for her directing, his smiles and laughter, his questions about her modeling training, were all aimed at ingratiating himself into her good favor. Oh, Elizabeth, thought Ann, you will soon know the truth. As Ann entered the room, Elizabeth welcomed her.

"Come on in. We're having great fun. Have you been to New Shore?" And she turned to explain to William, "Our sister and family are staying at New Shore, and Ann has been visiting Marie Smith, an old friend there."

At the name Marie Smith, William paled visibly and turning to Ann asked, "Marie Smith? Is she from Detroit?"

"No. She's from Chicago and her name is Maria, Maria Smith Brown." Ann tried to sound smoothly casual, and her deception seemed to succeed because William regained his composure, and the rehearsal continued.

Ann left for New Shore. She needed to confer with Marie again and enlist the help of Charles for the next stage of their plan.

Chapter XXIV

Many years ago, when the French owned all of the Great Lakes, there lived in a little village west of Mackinac a miller whose daughter was the prettiest in the territory. Her name was Marie Therese, and although she was promised to her most ardent admirer, Pierre, she was reminded every day of her beauty by many admirers who came to her door with gifts of flowers or ribbons and poetic words, trying to win her heart.

The fortune teller, Mere Minique, had told her she could delay marriage in order to enjoy more parties and travel to the big city of Quebec. She should watch for a wealthy stranger who would take her away to live in a grand chateau where she would have fine gowns and attend fancy balls with the most important people of the land.

On Mardi Gras night, Pierre came for her in his sleigh to take her to the biggest dance of the season. As she left the house, her mother warned, "Remember, this is the beginning of Lent, and you must stop dancing at midnight and leave for home immediately or something terrible will happen."

The couple laughed and left with the assurance that they would soon return. At the party Marie was having the time of her life, but unhappy Pierre could hardly dance with her because of the throng of her admirers. When the clock struck twelve, he begged for one more dance. The fiddlers promised one more tune, but before he could lead Marie to the floor, the door opened, and a tall dark stranger entered, asking permission to warm himself and to keep his hat on because of the cold night. He was very distinguished looking with lace at his throat and wrists. Everyone welcomed him, and he bowed before Marie, asking her to dance.

Pierre was angry. He stomped outside to bring his horse and sleigh to the door. But there he saw the stranger's horse and sleigh and noticed something odd. In spite of the cold, the snow around the horse's hooves had melted. There were bare spots on the ground around each hoof. Pierre, suddenly realizing why the stranger had kept his hat and gloves on, ran to fetch the priest.

As Pierre and the priest entered the dance hall, they heard the stranger say, "Come with me," and saw Marie reach out her hand to him. But as her hand touched the stranger's hand, his claws pierced her skin. Drops of blood appeared in her palm, and she fell to the floor in a faint. The Devil-stranger leaned to pick her up, but the priest jumped between them holding up the cross.

"She is mine," roared the Devil. "She has made a compact in blood."

"No, she belongs to God," said the priest. "She is promised for the convent. Look at this cross I hold before you."

The Devil took one look, howled with a hideous voice, and disappeared in a cloud of smoke.

Henrietta was standing in front of the room telling this story as the players acted out the scenes she described. She was wearing a long white Cinderella gown and a tiny gold tiara. Louisa was the doomed Marie Therese, with her blond curls concealed under a long dark wig and wearing a green calico dress with a lace shawl. Charles, as the

Devil, was attired in a ridiculous top hat and long coat. As the story drew to an end, he was relieved to pull off the lace fichu which was scratching his neck.

Adam enjoyed being the priest, garbed in a long black choir robe and holding up the huge crucifix. And Ben, as the disappointed Pierre, was eager to run and grab his sweetheart in a rescuing embrace.

"Wait! Stop!" Henrietta shouted. "You're getting ahead of the story. According to the voyageur storytellers, the priest led Marie Therese off to a convent and the sad Pierre went away to join the French Marines, never to be seen again. But we have changed the story for a more realistic and happy true ending. In real life Pierre claims Marie Therese as his bride, (Go ahead. You can kiss her now.) and they have instructed me to tell you that these two actors, in real life, Captain Benjamin Benwick, and Miss Louisa Musgrove, hereby announce their engagement to be married!"

Laughter, applause, and expressions of surprise followed the announcement. People crowded around the actors to give them congratulations on the success of the skit and wishes of happiness for the engaged couple.

One of the most surprised, and not a little pleased, was Ann. Louisa and Ben? A most unlikely pair, she surmised. But was their commitment the cause of Frederick's comment about "fickle women"? How disappointed was he really, if at all?

Her speculation that Frederick was the jilted one was enforced by the fact that he had not come to the ball. Ann had looked for him in vain.

The evening had begun in splendid fashion with a grand march led by Jewell and Henry Von Russett. Jewell was Queen Elizabeth I with ropes of pearls and a huge hooped skirt. Henry was dressed as his own ancestor, Diedrich Knickerbocker, complete with the eponymous britches and the buckled shoes.

Elizabeth and Penny appeared to be dressed in non-descript old-fashioned men's clothing until they turned around to reveal signs on their backs identifying them as Meriwether Lewis and William Clark. To the frequently asked question, "Where is Sacajawea?" they answered, "Wait and see."

A group of fine musicians played such a variety of selections that every dancer was sooner or later pleased with the music, and the crowd of oddly-mixed, costumed couples added to the mirth of the occasion and made observing from the sidelines as entertaining as dancing.

William Eliot, as Antoine Cadillac in his plumed hat, and Elizabeth, with her long blonde hair swinging around her high-collared coat, were the center of attraction during the waltzes. They shared the limelight with Admiral and Mrs. Croft who came as a British admiral and his Regency wife, looking like characters right out of a Jane Austen novel.

Ann's decidedly un-feminine voyageur costume was no deterrent to attracting dance partners. Her first was a tall gentleman wearing a giant papier mache head modeled after Michigan's governor. Conversation with him was a definite challenge because he had to keep his head very erect and his voice came through the mask in a hollow mumble.

Her next partner was her Uncle Henry, who made up in liveliness what he lacked in rhythm. His buckled shoes had heavy wooden heels which he clacked and clumped loudly on the polished floor.

She tried several times to make her way

through the crowd to the Admiral in order to inquire if Frederick had received her message, or if he planned to come to the party, but each time she approached them, either she or they became involved in the next dance.

A contra dance was announced, and Ann found herself paired with Charles Musgrove. He had removed his devil's hat, but he still wore a severe expression. He was truly agitated. "I'm worried that our villain may suspect something. The plan was for Marie to identify him, and Frederick is to bring a man to serve the warrant for his arrest, but Frederick isn't here yet. Can you delay Marie when she comes?"

It was too late! Marie appeared in the doorway. She was not Hiawatha, but Sacajawea. A real baby, her own, rode in a sling on her back. Her Indian costume of leather-like dress had beaded fringe, and her long dark wig was held in place with a colorful band. Lewis and Clark naturally gravitated toward her, but as the music paused, she announced in a clear voice, "This is not really my Indian baby. This is the Red Dwarf." And taking the child from her back, she revealed a toddler dressed all in red and wearing a red bonnet. Amid laughter and applause, she led the child toward the front of the hall where William Eliot stood and said, "Monsieur Cadillac will undoubtedly recognize this dwarf."

There was more laughter and applause. Of course, it was the mother he recognized, in spite of the wig and costume. Monsieur Cadillac stiffened suddenly, but only Ann and a few others noticed his extreme discomfiture. He recovered his aplomb and managed to resume his proper role. "Yes, you are Nain Rouge, but I will not hit you with my cane."

He was spared further embarrassment by the sound of a loud gong calling everyone to the dining room, and in the shuffle of departing dancers, he was separated from the mother and child and was able to escape any conversation or accusation from Marie. There was no suspicion on the part of anyone else that a very shocking recognition had taken place.

Chapter XXV

Most of the tables seated four each, and because Ann waited for Marie, they found a table near the door.

As they were sitting down, Ann heard, "May we join you?" It was Frederick, in his Coast Guard uniform and Joe Gish, an Island police officer, in mufti.

Flustered and pleased, Ann welcomed them and introduced Marie and the child.

"Where is he?" asked Frederick. "We can't stay. Point him out to us."

Just then, Charles hurried up to their table. "Quick, toward the front of the hall." Joe and Frederick followed him, but they were too late. Billy Oxbridge, alias William Eliot, had disappeared.

The three men returned toward the door and as they passed Ann's table, Frederick whispered urgently, "Help us, Ann!" and she jumped up to follow them.

While Charles searched restrooms and hallways, Joe Gish obtained the key to William's room, and they entered it to find only the costume coat and big hat. The window was open, and because it gave directly onto a fire escape, they hurried down it, hoping to find him in the gardens.

Joe stopped them to give instructions for a more organized search. "Frederick, you check the dock. He'll most likely try to get off the island. I'll bike to the office and get flashlights."

But Ann reminded them, "The last ferry to the mainland left twenty minutes ago. He couldn't have made it to the dock before then."

"New Shore resort has their own speedboat for late departures," Charles added. "I'll check there."

They finally settled on the plan to meet back at the Grand Hotel after Charles had checked the New Shore dock and Ann and Frederick had tried the road to the Woodsy Restaurant.

Frederick knew where the bicycles were kept in back of the hotel but found them all securely locked, so he and Ann started a slow jog toward the Woodsy. There was no moon, and after they left the lights of the hotel grounds, only faint starlight gave indication of the road.

"He could be hiding anywhere along here in the trees," Frederick said.

Ann did not agree. "I think he'll head for a public place and ask for help with some plausible story. He'll think of something. What a deceiver!"

"You don't know the half of it. The investigation turned up more dirt than you know. He has played the game of 'marry the rich widow' several times with a different identity each time. He is actually Bartholomew Tonti, wanted in England for the suspected murder of his friend who was the real William Eliot."

"Wow! William Eliot was supposed to be bringing a friend here. No one here knew him, so it was easy to fool us. But we'd have had the last laugh, anyway. The Michigan Eliots are no longer wealthy and both Elizabeth and I were suspecting that he was some kind of fake. We're lucky that Marie decided to work on the Island again this summer. What a discovery!"

The Woodsy was closing, and the manager on duty said that no one of William Eliot's description had come in.

As they left, heading down toward the shore road, Ann related the race-day incident to Frederick, explaining why she had not waited for him at the finish line.

They were nearing the hotel. "And who is the person I knew five years ago who wanted to talk with me?"

Ann stopped. Frederick stopped. They looked at each other, coming closer in the darkness. "Can't you guess?" she asked.

"I was hoping…"

"Ann! Frederick!" It was Charles calling to them. He and Joe ran toward them. Joe was carrying a monstrous flashlight and Charles was holding the leash, at the end of which bounded the big bloodhound. "I brought Trapper. I'm sure if she gets the proper whiff, she can lead us to Eliot. Let's go back to his room and pick up that jacket to use for scent. I haven't been training Trapper all this time for nothing."

A few minutes later, a vacationing couple

who were taking a late night walk from a downtown hotel were startled by a strange sight. "Did you see that?" the woman asked. "A man with a devil suit and someone in a coonskin cap."

"It looked like one guy had a gun and a pair of handcuffs."

"The dog was really going, and that sailor was following along with a big flashlight."

"Crazy college kids. Must be a weird kind of treasure hunt."

About an hour later the motley search team arrived at the top of the island, in front of a cave. Joe cautioned the others to stay back while he went toward the cave entrance and called out,

"You are under arrest! Come out with your hands up."

"Call off the dog," came the answer. "I'm coming out!"

Trapper was only a tracking dog, not an attack dog, but her size was intimidating and had conveyed the proper effect for apprehending a felon. William Eliot, no longer the dapper charmer, emerged from the low entrance of the cave, disheveled, coatless and shivering, covered with dirt, his lace fichu torn, and his expression one of angry defeat. But he submitted to the manacles and began the forced march down the hill. Because the flashlight was focused on him only, he was not aware that Ann was part of the entourage.

Joe made a radio call on the way, alerting the Coast Guard Utility boat waiting in the harbor that they were on their way with their suspect. The descent was more rapid than the climb up had been. Ann and Frederick found themselves in the rear, again carrying on a hurried conversation in brief spurts.

"I wanted you to know that I found your letter on my payroll check receipt in Aunt Nettie's papers."

"She never sent it on or told you?"

"I had told her to deposit my check directly to my bank account. You never received my postcard?"

"It probably came after I left that summer. Nothing got forwarded to me."

"I'm so sorry."

"We need more time to talk. We need to catch up. With my Coast Guard duties I have 'one foot on shore, and one at sea,' but I want to convince you that I am not like the guy in the poem; how did it go? 'To one thing never constant'?"

"You read the e-mail I sent to the Admiral?"

"I was the one answering you at his computer! Do you believe that other poem about 'not removing with the remover'?"

They were nearing the lights of the village and headed toward the dock. Ann's reply sounded rather breathless, not from their rapid pace, but from her emotional agitation.

"Oh, yes. Do you?"

Frederick did not answer the question directly, but as a reply, stopped and took a small object from his pocket, grabbed her hand and pressed the object into it, closing her fingers over what felt like a key ring and chain. As he hurried onto the boat behind Officer Gish and the prisoner, he called out, "I hope you remember this. I'll be back."

Ann, Charles, and Trapper stood on the dock watching the lights of the boat and its white wake fade in the distance. Ann looked at the key ring in her hand. It was the other half of the Petoskey stone he had given her during their Island summer together, now polished and enclosed in a little gold cage attached to the tiny chain.

Chapter XXVI

That night Ann slept soundly and content. It was strange that since the disappearance of the green-label box, Julio had not slept on the stack of boxes, even though Ann had re-stacked them to arrange his customary perch. He now preferred to sleep on the foot of Ann's bed. During the night she was visited by the familiar dream. But this time instead of stopping at the closed door, Aunt Nettie opened it, entered the room, and came toward Ann, looking down at her with a pleasant smile.

Ann awoke and wondered at the open door to her room. She was sure she had closed it before going to bed. Then in the darkness she heard the door slowly closing. She heard the click of the latch and the sound of steps as if someone were descending the stairway. She turned on the light and saw Julio on the floor staring at the door.

She opened the door, thinking he perhaps wanted out, but the cat jumped back onto the bed, as if the visitor were not worth following.

The presence of the ghost, if that is what it was, did not frighten her. She had the comforting feeling that perhaps the spirit of Aunt Nettie was now satisfied. A poor judgment made five years ago had been remedied for the happiness of all concerned.

The revelation of the true character of William Eliot was a mild surprise for Elizabeth and Penny, a startling amazement to Henry, but an astounding shock to Jewell. She had been so thoroughly charmed by his suave manner that she was at first unwilling to believe the proof of his deception. Her hopes of adding to the family a fine young man with the name of Eliot were crushed. The fact that neither Elizabeth nor Ann regretted the loss did not lessen her own disappointment, a large measure of which was due to the embarrassment at her own poor judgment. Her first reaction was to conceal the fact from general knowledge. But the weekly Island newspaper somehow found the scandal worthy of front page coverage under the headline DOG IS HERO IN APPREHENDING FELON, accompanied by a large photo of Trapper. Jewell was grateful that only the feet of Charles appeared in the photo, and that there was no photo available of the criminal, who was being exdradited to England on charges of fraud and suspicion of murder.

She was so overcome by the shame of the whole business that she pulled the front curtains shut, retired to her room, and left instructions with Tomkins that she was "Not at home, but you may leave your card" to any caller who came by.

Jewell's recovery from this disaster was promoted by two revelations. The first was that Frederick Wentworth was still in love with Ann, and after five years could no longer be considered merely a frivolous passing acquaintance. Further proof of his eligibility came when she discovered that his family actually owned a controlling interest in both the Grand Hotel and New Shore Resort. The Wentworths were a family of means indeed! Her error in misjudging the character of Frederick was much easier to recover from than that of her previous assessment of William Eliot. At this time,

Jewell's only bar to happiness was the problem of how to decline a gift graciously, the offer of one of Trapper's expected puppies.

So Frederick was invited to dinner at Bluff Cottage, and Jewel was prepared to welcome him and approve of his manners, appearance and friendship with Ann. But on the morning of the planned dinner party there was a revelation that was more devastating to Jewel than even the exposure of William Eliot had been.

Ann had long suspected that the relationship between Elizabeth and Penny was more than friendship, but there had been no acknowledgement on their part that it was more than a sisterly affection. Elizabeth, after breakfast that morning, calmly announced that she and Penny were moving to Chicago, where Elizabeth was taking employment as a teacher in a modeling and charm school.

"And," she added, "Penny and I are planning to adopt a little boy."

Shock upon shock for poor Jewell! "What do you mean, you and Penny?"

"We're married, Aunt Jewell, at least in our own minds. Have you noticed our rings?" And they placed their left hands together on the table before her, displaying their identical silver rings worn on the third finger.

The name of their kind of relationship was so abhorrent to Jewell that she could not pronounce the word.

Henry broke the stunned silence which followed the announcement by saying, "Well, I guess a kid can have two mothers as long as he has uncles and grandfathers."

"And he'll have a big brother. Penny has gained custody of her little boy, and we'll be quite a family," added Elizabeth.

"An old-fashioned conventional family, almost," added Penny, "because I'm to be the stay-at-home mom while Elizabeth is the working mom."

Ann offered her congratulations and asked when the adoption would take place. There were legal difficulties and obstacles to such unions, but Penny's father, a man well experienced with the law, had been working to smooth the details and by October everything would be settled.

The shock to Jewell was so devastating that she not only closed the front curtains and declared herself not at home; she also took to her bed with a throbbing headache and decided she would never come out. Though still reeling from the blow, she did decide to come down for dinner, but she could not bring herself to mention the matter or to look directly at Elizabeth and Penny.

Her recovery was aided by the fact that the two women would be leaving Bluff Cottage, and the situation need not be acknowleged publicly at all. She would be spared the embarrassment and shame of admitting such an unconventional, indeed such a sinful situation, existed in her own family. She was again thankful that her sister Nettie had been spared this disclosure. If she had not already died, the revelation of this relationship would have killed her, absolutely!

During the dinner Jewell was stiff and silent. Henry made a valiant attempt to lighten the mood, and with Penny's laughter at his jokes, he succeeded fairly well. Frederick appeared to fit in comfortably and added his own stories to the entertainment of the family. Mrs. Tomkins had cooked her Upper Michigan specialty, Welsh "pasties," the individual meat and vegetable servings, folded in baked pastry.

Frederick complimented her cuisine, but spent most of his time between bites looking at Ann. She returned his gaze with happy smiles as if they shared a special secret.

Ann asked to be excused from the table so that she and Frederick could take their dessert and coffee later, as they wanted to take a run before dark, and the two started off along the shore road beyond the West Bluff. The run became a slow jog, then finally a walk, and ended on a solitary stretch of road with a warm embrace.

Then followed a conversation which cleared up all the misunderstandings of the past and recalled the feelings of each during the intervening years since they had met. Ann expressed her regrets at not having persisted in trying to contact him.

Frederick explained how his association with Louisa had become an embarrassment, and admitted that her accident had brought home to him the error of encouraging an attraction which was quite hollow. They agreed that Louisa and Ben seemed to be very different in their personalities, but a similarity of interests, added to that special chemistry which makes so many couples come together, would ensure an enduring marriage.

He also admitted that jealousy of William Eliot had almost ruined his hopes for regaining Ann. Never had a man been so triumphant in defeating a rival, as Frederick was in the capture and arrest of William Eliot.

Ann took the little Petoskey stone and the key ring from her pocket and showed him how the two halves matched.

Frederick said, "Let's trade. You keep the key ring and I'll have this half of the stone made into another one for me."

The conversation ended with long kisses and a plan to meet at the Bridge Walk on Labor Day. A slim crescent moon was setting, leaving the skies dark enough to reveal the northern lights.

"Look," she said. "Gitchie Manitou is smiling at us. That means we will live happily ever after."

The day of the Bridge Walk dawned warm and sunny. The brisk breeze did not deter any of the hundreds of people ready to cross from the Upper to the Lower Peninsula. Several buses had brought loads of people over from the south side, so that when traffic was halted, all would be walking in the same direction. The Von Russett-Eliot family were in merry spirits, and it would be difficult to say who was the happiest.

Perhaps it was Henry because he had elected to stay at home and watch with his telescope from Bluff Cottage. He congratulated himself at avoiding a five-mile walk in a crush of people.

Jewell felt gratified to be walking only five steps behind the Governor and his wife, as it signified to her that she had at last achieved the status due to her in the ranks of Island society.

Elizabeth and Penny walked hand-in-hand with shining eyes and the happy anticipation of the arrival of Baby Bobby.

But perhaps Ann was happiest of all as she marched along with Frederick. He had arrived late, and almost missed her in the group of people getting off the ferry.

When he spotted her in the crowd, he ran toward her and presented her with a little box. Inside was a ring made from her half of the Petoskey stone.

"It's not a diamond, but I thought you'd like this kind of engagement ring. It's made in the shape of a turtle, so we'll remember where we met."

"I love it," she replied. "Now, we trade again. Here's the key ring for you to carry. Let's run ahead so we can find the others. I want to show Jewell and Elizabeth."

And so our romance ends with promise of future happiness for all. What about Jewell's attitude toward Elizabeth and Penny? She was gradually reconciled to the idea. After such an ungracious delay as she owed to her own dignity, she consented to give her approval, if not her complete blessing, to the union of the two women. Her decision was endorsed by the appearance in October of the chubby baby himself with his large dark eyes, the fact that she would be loved as "Grandmama," and of no small importance, the fact that in his person the grand name of Eliot would be carried forward to the next generation.

FINIS

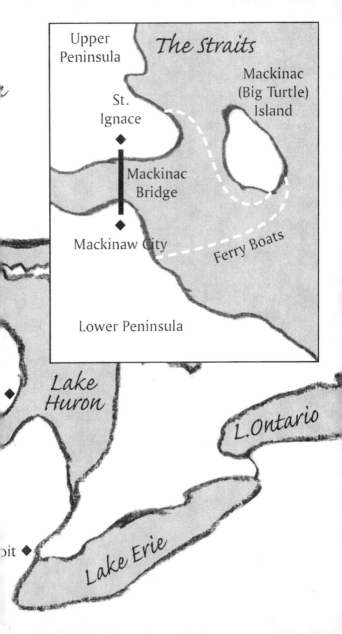